Back pg. wrinkled 7/14 DJ

10.

Discarded by
Santa Maria Library

Hancock Park

Hancock Park

Isabel Kaplan

HARPER TEEN

An Imprint of HarperCollins Publishers

Library of Congress Cataloging-in-Publication Data
Kaplan, Isabel.
    Hancock Park / Isabel Kaplan. — 1st ed.
        p.   cm.
    Summary: While attending an exclusive prep school in Los
Angeles, a smart but anxiety-ridden high school junior tries to deal
with boys, popularity, and her parents' divorce.
    ISBN 978-0-06-124652-4 (trade bdg.)
    [1. Preparatory schools—Fiction.   2. High schools—Fiction.
3.   Schools—Fiction.   4.   Anxiety—Fiction.   5.   Divorce—Fiction.
6. Popularity—Fiction.   7. Los Angeles (Calif.)—Fiction.]   I. Title.
PZ7.K1292Han   2009   2009005481
[Fic]—dc22   CIP
                                                      AC

Typography by Jennifer Heuer
09 10 11 12 13   LP/RRDB   10 9 8 7 6 5 4 3 2 1
❖
First Edition

For my parents.

On the Bright Side

*M*y name is Becky Miller, and my life is insane.

I should be looking at the glass as half full, though. Right? That's what my mom says.

Okay, so: Before Rite Aid called about my abnormally strong antidepressant prescription, before Grandma came to visit, before the whole situation with my parents, before Amanda left town, before the Trinity, before Aaron . . . things were kind of normal.

Or maybe they weren't. What is "normal" in Los Angeles, anyway?

Okay. Glass half full. On the bright side . . . I'm now a blonde.

My, Grandma,
What a Small Waist You Have

I awoke that Tuesday morning when a faint tapping gradually became not so faint and I realized that it wasn't just in my dreams. Someone was pounding at the front door. "Mom, I think she's here," I called out, sitting up in bed. The tapping switched to the doorbell. Then the doorbell rang again. Our doorbell isn't one of those pretty-sounding ones. It's obnoxiously generic. "Do you want me to get it?"

I heard a crash, and then Grandma's voice rang out clearly through the house. "Is anyone alive in there? I've been standing out here for at least two minutes! I see your cars in the driveway; don't think you can fool me!"

It had been this way for a week now. Grandma—Mom's mother—had insisted on staying in a hotel as opposed to staying with us, but every morning, bright and early, she took a taxi over to our house. I had only seven days before eleventh grade started. These were the final mornings of my summer vacation, and all I wanted was to be able to sleep late.

Clearly, Grandma had other ideas. Fortunately, this was the last day of her visit. She had spent most of the week with my mom, which was beyond fine with me. I usually waited for my mom to call me down to say hello, but that day, the shrillness of Grandma's voice sent me running—it was like a fight-or-flight thing. Mom and Jack, my thirteen-year-old brother, met me in the upstairs hallway. Jack was wearing only his boxers and held up a plastic sword, as if in defense. "I'm not going down there," he said. My mom was half dressed, her hair up in curlers.

"I can't let her see me looking like this," she told me. "Please, Becky? Just open the door?" In my wrinkled tank top and boxers, I wasn't looking so hot myself right then. I gave her a "You owe me" look, and she sprinted back toward her room. "I'll be down in a minute, I promise!" she called out to me.

Smoothing my hair a little, I headed down the stairs, refusing Jack's offer of the sword for protection. At the bottom step, I stopped and took a moment to gather myself. The little peek-through window in the middle of our front door had been pushed open, revealing—her face twisted in between the iron grates, Chanel sunglasses askew—my grandmother.

"Rebecca!" She moved back from the door as I moved forward to open it.

"It's Becky, Grandma," I reminded her for the millionth time. "Grandma's here!" I directed my voice upstairs. As if they didn't know already.

My grandmother ran her acrylic nails over our new front hall table, no doubt inspecting it as if deciding whether to give her approval. Next, she lifted her sunglasses up over her head and gave me a once-over for the same reason. "You know, I'd been wondering what changed with you— you look different this trip—and I've realized it's that you really aren't as chubby as you were when I last saw you." Grandma nodded and walked over to me. I winced as she grabbed my upper arm as if I were a cut of meat and felt for fat. "You're finally thinning out."

And you, I thought, *are an anorexic jerk.*

I know that's not a nice thought to have about your grandma, but it's not unwarranted.

The last time Grandma Elsie had visited was four years earlier, when I was twelve. Back then, Grandma, who did one independent film forty years ago and fancies herself a star, had talked a lot about how I was too chubby. "Kathy," she told my mother while I sat listening, unnoticed, behind the kitchen door, "you should really think about watching Rebecca's food intake. She's looking a little *zaftig*. Speaking of weight, Kathy," Grandma had added, referring to my mother, who was never any larger than a size 4, "I didn't realize that you were *gaining*. You look as though you've put on at least three pounds." She hadn't visited since, which was also beyond fine by me. I wasn't exactly sure why she was here now. She claimed to be helping my mother with something—with what, I had no idea.

Grandma was running her fake fingernails along the newly refinished banister. "Your mother isn't still asleep, is she?"

"Of course not, Mother." My mom glided down the stairs, her hair curled and her body wrapped in a dress that left little breathing room. Her smile was tight and forced. Jack followed behind her, still holding the sword.

"Good morning." Grandma nodded at Mom and turned her attention to Jack, who was gripping the sword in front of him. "My *kindelach*!" Elsie opened her arms wide, as if she were expecting Jack to run into them. Mom gave Jack a nudge, and he trudged forward to receive his punishment. "And Harold? Where is Harold today?"

"Harold!" Mom called up the stairs for my dad. "My mother's here." Every morning of Grandma's visit was a big production; day after day, she acted as if she hadn't seen us in years. We all waited a moment, silent and expectant, watching the top of the stairs and waiting for Dad to appear. Finally, he did, with his briefcase in one hand and his BlackBerry in the other.

"Right here. Good morning, Elsie." He walked down the stairs typing, and my mom nudged him and whispered something into his ear. Then, he held his arms out as he walked toward Grandma, as if to initiate a hug.

Grandma dismissed his invitation, dropping her hands to her sides. "Likewise." She smiled politely. After placing an overstuffed shoulder bag on the ground, she clapped her hands together. "Alright. Well, who wants to come shopping with me?" Grandma placed both hands around her minuscule waist and nodded toward my mother and me. From my position behind her, I placed my hands on my own waist and did an elaborate imitation of her mannerisms, sticking my chin up in the air and smirking. Mom stifled a chuckle and shot me a sharp look.

Dad straightened his tie and headed to the front door. "Wish I could, really, but I have to head to work. I'll see you all tonight." He pulled the door shut behind him.

Jack let out a laugh. "*I* don't wish I could. Sorry, G-ma. I don't do shopping." Nobody responded, so he made a quick exit toward the kitchen. Now, it was just me, Mom, and Grandma standing in the front hall. Mom fingered the hem of her dress. It was now or never.

I took an extended glance at the clock, sighed, and said, "Oh, would you look at that . . ." but Mom walked toward me, her eyes wide, pleading.

"I . . ." I clenched my hands, counted to three, then clenched my hands twice more. I could have said no. I wanted to say no. But I didn't. I care too much about pleasing people.

I forced a smile toward Grandma. "Where did you want to go shopping?"

Mom grabbed her purse off the front hall table and came to stand next to me. Whispering in my ear, she said, "Thank you so much, sweetheart. That Ron Herman sweatshirt you wanted? *Yours.* I'll go get it for you this afternoon on my way back from Brentwood." She put her arm around me and looked at her mother. "I really have to get to work, but Becky will take you shopping this morning. She has plans this afternoon, though." Mom winked at me. "Right?"

I nodded.

I went upstairs to change but wasn't sure what to wear for a day of probable torture with Grandma. I settled on a basic if slightly preppy outfit: a frayed denim miniskirt with a light pink polo shirt. Grandma examined me from beneath her sunglasses as I reemerged in the front hall. I examined her right back, wondering how she and my mom could possibly be related. Grandma lives for leopard print, zebra print, and, well, any print in general. And she wears them all together. My mom, on the other hand, is a style guru. Really—she has her own TV show. To her, mixing animal prints is cause for an intervention.

"Jack, we're leaving!" I called as we headed out the front door. "We'll be back soonish." I hope. "If you need anything, call me on my cell." I shut the door behind me and stepped out into the already bright summer sun.

Grandma stood in front of my red Volkswagen Jetta, tapping her feet. As I clicked the UNLOCK button on my car key, two large golden retrievers leaped toward me, dragging Nancy Clarke, a middle-aged woman in tennis whites, behind them. "Becky, darling, how are you?" Nancy skidded to a stop on the sidewalk.

"I'm great. Nancy, this is my grandma, Elsie." I turned to Grandma, who was busy examining her face in a compact. "Grandma, this is Nancy Clarke. The Clarkes live a couple blocks over, on Hudson."

At least for the next few days they did. My best friend, Amanda Clarke, and her family were just two days away from moving across the country so that Amanda's dad could pursue "a new challenge" for his directorial career: Broadway.

Nancy put her hand on my back and smiled. "It's good to meet you, Elsie." She extended her hand. Grandma snapped the compact shut and, wordlessly, shook Nancy's hand, then turned to open the passenger door and folded her tiny body into the seat.

I stepped forward and spoke quickly, eager to rectify Grandma's dismissive attitude. "Great to run into you! We're going shopping now. Have a good walk! I'm sure I'll see you soon," I called out as I headed toward the driver's side of the car. Nancy still stood on the sidewalk, the dogs pulling at her, but after I flashed a smile and opened the car door, she gave a wave and headed off. I drove toward Beverly Boulevard, took a deep breath, and addressed Grandma. "Where to?"

"Why don't we do Barneys?"

Grandma fiddled with the radio buttons, and as a light turned yellow, I slowed to a stop. "It's yellow! That means hurry up! You can go!" she shrieked, banging on the dashboard with her hands. I pushed down on the brake a little harder.

As we drove through Beverly Hills, Grandma's face was glued to the window, but her hands remained firmly folded in her lap. "Camden Drive! I know that street from somewhere . . . is that where that new hot boutique is? I think I read about it in *Us Weekly* last month."

"No. That's where my dentist is," I replied. No hot boutique. Unless you count it as the hotbed of celebrity teeth whitening. Of course, I didn't say that out loud. I turned into the Barneys New York lot, left my car keys at the valet stand, and wondered if other grandmothers read *Us Weekly* and tried to keep up on the "hot boutiques." How had this woman spawned my mother, who, despite being part of the Hollywood thing, didn't really care much about it?

Grandma marched ahead of me toward the large black-and-white-striped awning. Gusts of air-conditioning blew at us as we entered the building, stepping onto the mirrored tile floors. Behind the first-floor makeup and fragrance counters, salespeople clad all in black smiled brightly, vying for attention and credit cards. Grandma approached the MAC makeup counter. She picked up a small pot of turquoise eye shadow and dabbed some on her palm. She was using her fingers, which is highly unsanitary, and I hoped that nobody was watching.

"Did you know," I said to her as I fiddled with the cap of a lip gloss, "that department stores like Barneys put the products that sell best on the first floor? They make more money from lip gloss and perfume than they do from Marc Jacobs!" I don't think that Grandma even caught the end of my sentence because when I turned around, she was standing all the way across the store, arranging a plaid Burberry scarf around her neck.

But that fact, included as part of a speech, had helped Amanda win the gavel award at a Model United Nations conference this past spring. Model United Nations (or MUN to us MUN people) might sound like some geeky role-playing thing, but at Whitbread School for Girls, one of the best private schools in the country, we have a new slogan: "Not just pretending to solve world problems." Last year, Amanda and I were co-presidents of MUN, and our team not only won the California MUN tournament but also raised money to rebuild several schools that had been damaged by the 2005 earthquake in Pakistan.

Not that Grandma cared about any of that.

All she cared about right now was jeans. After she finally found a suitable pair, women's waist size 25, we headed up to the top floor of the store to Barney Greengrass. The elevator opened, and Grandma sighed with a smile of pleasure as she walked into the restaurant and waited for the hostess to approach us. I stepped forward reluctantly. Grandma would ask for "the best table in the house," and while that might work for her in Florida, it wouldn't fly here. Especially since she was dressed head to toe in leopard print.

"Hi." I smiled at the hostess. I glanced down at my lime green sneakers and clasped my hands behind my back trying to hide the anxiety I felt building. My psychiatrist says I should do my best to not let anxiety get the best of me. And if that doesn't work, well, there's always Xanax. "We'll be two today." If I said "today," she might think that I was a regular or even a once-in-a-while patron. Technically, I sort of was. I had been here once, in May, with my mom. Twice in three months counted as once in a while, right?

The hostess led us past Botoxed Beverly Hills women clinking glasses, as well as the occasional businessman or Hollywood type in suit and tie, to a table on the edge of the dining area, across from the pastry counter. It was a prime people-watching position, and Grandma was pleased. Except that once we had our menus and the waiter came over to take our orders, I immediately felt stupid for suggesting that we get something to eat. I had, of course, forgotten that my grandmother doesn't eat.

I ordered a grilled chicken sandwich and an iced tea. Grandma daintily closed her menu and glanced up at the waiter, who was running his hands through overly gelled hair. An actor. For sure. Maybe he thought Grandma was some quirky casting director. "You know, I am just not that hungry right now," she mused, patting her nonexistent belly. "I think I'll have a cup of tea." She paused. "Yes, a cup of hot tea sounds nice." While we waited for the food and tea to come, Grandma interrogated me about my love life and demanded that I explain why I didn't have a boyfriend. (Answers: *What love life?* and *The fact that the only boys I know are my teachers certainly doesn't help.*) She removed a cocktail ring that had been on her right hand and placed it on her ring finger. "I sure could use a man to put a real rock on my finger," she said.

Grandma has been married four times.

I swirled the straw in my iced tea and gave a small nod, biting my lip.

"Oh, Rebecca," Grandma sighed, adjusting the crystal frog pin in her blazer. She raised her voice and leaned back in the chair. "I really do need to find a man!" A table of chattering blondes to our left stopped their conversation to turn and stare at my grandmother. Horrified, I pushed my chair back and stood up, muttering something about needing to find more Equal. I walked to the pastry counter, and as I started to ask for Equal that I didn't actually want or need, a shrill voice erupted from behind me. "*Sheyne meydlech*, Re-*bec*-ca, your skirt is riding up in the back, sweetheart!"

My hands flew to the back of my denim skirt, and to

my relief, I found that the skirt was safely covering my behind. Grabbing the hem anyway, I pulled it downward and took a deep breath. I could have turned around, but the restaurant was fairly crowded, and I didn't really want to see any eyes on me.

I leaned in toward the woman behind the counter. "Could you, you know, maybe drop a plate or something? Just to divert the attention." She raised her eyebrows. "People are staring, aren't they?" She nodded.

Then, as I prepared to turn around and make my graceful return back to the table, I felt a hand on the small of my back. A small shiver went up my spine, and when I looked up to see to whom that hand belonged, the shiver became something more of a shock. "I think the skirt is very attractive. It's not riding up in the least." Nicholas Hargrove winked at me.

"Thank you." I swiveled my body around, hoping to remove his middle-aged hand from my back.

Grandma's mouth dropped open as she stared at the scene unfolding. Movie stars aren't as common in Del Ray Beach, Florida. She was out of earshot. I knew it must be killing her.

I took a step back, trying to distance myself. Nicholas recovered quickly from my dismissal. He smoothed out his blazer and flashed a several-thousand-dollar smile.

"Nicholas Hargrove," he said, holding out his hand.

So he was one of *those* celebrities. The type who introduce themselves, as if you don't already know who they are.

Problem is, this celebrity seemed to be forgetting that we had, in fact, met before. Several times. I hesitated just a moment too long, my hands firmly planted in the pockets of my skirt. Nicholas winked at me, and when he winked, wrinkles around his eyes appeared, nicely complementing his just-beginning-to-gray, too-old-for-me hair.

Should I do it?

This was the moment of truth. His hand was outstretched in front of me. Grandma's toes were tapping, knees bouncing, excitedly.

"Becky Miller." I inserted my hand into his. We shook, and he held on for just a moment too long. "Your daughter, Alissa, is in my class at Whitbread. We're going to be juniors—pretty exciting, huh? Only two more years of high school left!" I added, flashing my brightest smile.

He dropped my hand and his smile disappeared. "I . . . uh . . . it's, um, good to see you, Becky! Yes, juniors, how exciting. . . ." Nicholas nodded his head and took a step back, still facing me. "You have a good day now." He spun on his heels and walked back toward the table that he had been occupying.

"Your Equal?" The woman behind the counter handed me several little blue packages, and I thanked her. "Now that," she added, chuckling and nodding her head toward Nicholas Hargrove, "was funny."

I walked back to Grandma and sat down. My food had arrived, and Grandma was sipping her tea and reaching across the table, taking french fries off my plate. "Do you want me to put some on a plate for you?" I asked her.

"No, no," she told me, grabbing another handful. "I'm not hungry." She craned her neck, trying to find Nicholas. "You know something?" I knew it was rhetorical, so I didn't respond. "Your mother needs a good man. What about *him*?"

Pulling my plate toward me, out of her reach, I gave her a pointed look. "My mom is married, Grandma."

Take Me Away

I'd always wanted to be just like my mom. (Especially when I learned she got a perfect score on her SATs. I was much more likely to follow in her footsteps in the brains department than in the looks department, anyway.) And even though I was sixteen and probably supposed to hate my parents, that hadn't changed. She and I had always been close. She told me everything—maybe too much sometimes—so even after Grandma made that comment, I couldn't believe there might have been something going on in our family that Mom hadn't shared with me. I didn't want to flat-out ask her what was going on—although she shared (and overshared) with me, that's not how our relationship worked. She always told, but I never asked. So instead I launched a subtle offensive.

"And then, after all that," I told my mom that night, "she suggested that you need a good man and that *Nicholas Hargrove* might be that man!"

Grandma had just been dropped off at the airport; Dad was still at work, and I was regaling Mom with tales of the day. We sat in the living room, talking above the sound effects coming from the video game in Jack's upstairs bedroom.

"Can you believe it? I had to remind her that you're *married*." I looked up, trying to gauge her response. My mom leaned forward, set her mug down on the dark wooden coffee table, sat up, and took a deep breath.

Oh, shit.

I shook my head and felt my stomach drop. "Mom?" My heart began to thump. "You . . ." I couldn't finish the sentence, couldn't form the words to the question that I wanted to ask. Instead, I left my eyes lingering hopefully on hers. She had on end-of-the-day remnants of TV makeup, which is just like regular makeup but ten times the thickness. Mom likes to joke that, after wearing the stuff every day, she now has a permanent inch-thick coating on her face. September would mark the one-year anniversary of her job as the host of *Kathy's Eye* on the Style & Design Network. Mom was really excited to get her own show (before, she had been a commentator on a couple of morning programs), but it seemed to me that she was much more tired lately. Tonight, her eyeliner was smeared and there were shadows under her usually bright blue eyes.

Finally, Mom said something. "I was thinking of taking up running. What do you think? Would you be interested in running with me?" She addressed the landscape painting above the fireplace behind me.

I stood up and felt for the cell phone in my pocket, my heart pounding heavily now. "I . . . have to go. I forgot that I have, um, plans."

"Sweetheart!" my mom called out. I had made it all the way across the room and was nearly at the front door. Her voice grew quieter. "Grandma shouldn't have said that. This isn't how we wanted you to find out. . . ."

Fuck.

"What's going on?" I whispered, holding the archway for support.

"This isn't how we wanted to tell you."

My eyes and throat began to burn, and I started to inch backward.

"Can I give you a hug?" she asked.

I wanted to escape before I started crying. Crying would make it seem like I couldn't handle it—make it seem like I was weak. I was supposed to be strong; I wanted to be strong. After I broke my wrist in the sixth grade, I cried all the way home from the hospital. Finally, Mom had turned to me and said, "Don't be a baby, Becky. You're stronger than this." I'd tried my hardest not to cry in front of my mom—or anyone for that matter—ever since that. And I'd done a pretty good job of it.

"Not right now. I have to go." I rushed out the door and into the sunlight, power walking down the cracked Hancock Park sidewalks that held so many childhood memories. The driveway. That was where I had taught Joey Michaels and Jack how to rollerblade, where we had bladed down our first "big" hill together. At the time, it had seemed like a mountain. That driveway was where Joey's mom, Pam, would honk the horn of her dark green Honda minivan when it was her turn to take us to school or the park or the zoo. We loved her car best because the cream leather seats were so worn in, and it always smelled like chamomile. Then there was that depression in the sidewalk in front of the Turkish consulate. Years ago, when El Niño hit and I was about to turn ten, Jack, Joey, and I had brought toy boats out and floated them in the sidewalk, in that crevice.

I hadn't seen much of Joey lately. We had been best friends when we were little, but once we hit middle school, I guess I replaced him with Amanda and he replaced me with a newfound love for computer programming.

The big crack right where the sidewalk met the grass of the Rosenzweig's front yard was where I had flipped over on my Razor scooter in the sixth grade and broken my right wrist. And the corner, well, that was where I had almost broken the heel on a pair of my mom's Jimmy Choos— not to mention an ankle. That was my first time wearing heels, really. It was before a seventh-grade dance, and I was walking from my house to Amanda's. I had wanted to just turn right around and go home and change into something a little less deadly, but my mom had looked so happy when she offered to let me wear her shoes. I didn't want to disappoint her. For a twelve-year-old used to Converse sneakers, those two blocks proved to be treacherous—but I managed. Now, once again, I couldn't go home because of my mom. But this time, this stretch of sidewalk was the comfort I needed.

911

*I*n all my years of therapy, I'd never had a "psychiatrist moment"—when you just know that something you're dealing with is worth making an emergency call. When Jack toppled my bookshelves, I spent two hours trying to repair the specific alphabetical order of my books before I gave up, crying on the floor of my bedroom; but I took several deep breaths and realized, *Nope, not a genuine psychiatric emergency.* When we were on vacation in Cabo San Lucas, Mexico, for Mom's fiftieth birthday, and she locked herself in the bathroom while my dad went out to drink, leaving Jack and me alone in the hotel room, I was halfway through dialing Sara Elder's number when I hung up, dug around in my purse, and took a Xanax instead.

But as I moved down my block, walking quickly to get away from my house and everything that might be going on inside of it, I thought, *This qualifies as a psychiatrist moment.* It was after five, so I decided on her emergency number. Much as I hated using it, this very well might be one of the biggest emergencies in my life so far.

The phone rang twice before someone on the other end picked up. "Sara Elder's office," the woman said. This wasn't actually her office, and the woman on the phone and I both knew that.

"Hi. This is Becky Miller. I'm calling for Sara Elder."

"Alright." The sound of popping gum crackled over the phone line. "What is your call concerning?"

I kicked my toe against a patch of grass along the edge of the sidewalk. "Do I have to tell you?"

"Well, no," the woman replied. "It's just information that the doctor likes to have."

"Just tell her that I need to speak with her, please."

"One moment." Music began to play as I was placed on hold. "Ms. Miller? I can't reach the doctor, but I paged her and left a message, and she will call you back shortly. Can I take down a number for you?"

I paused, standing at the edge of my block. Suddenly, I couldn't remember my area code. 323? 310? My mind was racing. Taking a deep breath, I tried to pull it together and gave her my number. I flipped the phone shut and turned the corner that led toward Amanda's house.

I walked down the block, gazing distractedly at the

large homes and sprawling front lawns that defined the neighborhood. Many of the houses in Hancock Park were built in the early 1900s—most had an East Coast, traditional architectural feel to them, but some were inspired by Spanish or Mediterranean themes. Thanks to a historical preservation act, homeowners were prohibited from buying one of these houses, tearing it down, and then building a new one.

I finally approached the Clarkes' 1920s-era Spanish-style house, but I hesitated before starting up the walkway. I wasn't actually sure why I was here, but I had walked off without my car, and there were only so many places (read: basically nowhere) that I could get to on foot. Amanda was my friend, my best friend since seventh grade, and although she'd be gone in a few days, she was here now. And I needed her. I rang the doorbell, my stomach flittering as I waited for someone to come to the door and wondered if I should've called first. To my great relief, Amanda—tall, gangly, and with her bright blonde hair in a ponytail—bounced down the stairs to greet me. "Hey! What's up? Oh—my mom said she ran into you and your grandmother this morning. This was her last day here, right?"

I nodded my head and Amanda grabbed a pile of mail from the front table and bounded up the stairs, climbing them two at a time. "I like the Christmas lights," I told her as I ran my fingers over the dusty, multicolored bulbs hanging from the banister.

"Funny," she replied. It was a running joke we had. The Clarkes had taken to leaving the Christmas lights up year-round because it made Christmas decorating in December less work. Although I guessed they wouldn't be needing them this year.

"So, what's up?" Amanda asked as we entered her room and she sorted through the mail.

"Nothing's up!" The words just came out. I'd come over here to vent, to lean on my friend while she was still here. I'd come over here because I had nowhere else to go. But I couldn't bring myself to say anything important. I was too used to keeping my problems to myself. "What's up with you?"

"Y'know." She nodded, looking around her room, which has half in boxes. "Are you . . . I mean, I just wasn't expecting you. Did you call earlier? My cell was off."

"Oh. Sorry, no, I . . . forgot . . . to call. I just had to get away from my Grandma, so I thought I'd come over." It was barely a lie. I did want to get away from Grandma—and fortunately, she'd just left. But Grandma wasn't all that I wanted to get away from.

"Grandparents," she said, rolling her eyes.

I wanted to tell her what was going on—I did—but I just couldn't make the words come out.

"No way." She held a large envelope with our maroon school crest on the front. "My schedule. Guess my mom forgot to tell them I wasn't coming. Just like she and my dad forgot to tell me we were *moving*." She sat down, cross-legged, on her trundle bed.

Amanda's dad's midcareer crisis–inspired decision to trade directing big movies for directing Broadway shows was not going over well with me and Amanda. She didn't want to leave, and I didn't want to be left.

"You're going to have such a great year, Bex."

Nobody called me Rebecca, but only Amanda called me Bex.

"How do you figure?" I asked, sinking down into her beanbag chair.

"Because you get to be here."

"What's so great about here?" I said. Frankly, I'd rather be anywhere but.

She lay down and looked over at me. "It's . . . here. It's L.A. It's, you know, home."

She wasn't trying to make me feel worse—she didn't even know how awful I was feeling to begin with—but each word buried me a little more. Here . . . L.A. . . . home.

"You'll be okay," I said, because that was what you were supposed to say when things sucked. Then, you were supposed to say, "Look on the bright side: At least . . ."

Look on the bright side: At least your crazy grandmother wasn't in town for an entire week.

Look on the bright side: At least your little brother isn't a freak of nature.

Look on the bright side: At least your parents aren't getting divorced.

But I didn't say that. Just thinking it made my insides feel like they were caught in my throat. So I stopped thinking it, and then I was floating, in the sky, on the ceiling, barely hanging onto the crystal chandelier, just a shadow of myself, watching the scene unfold below. It felt just like sixth grade, when Sara Elder prescribed me sleeping pills that made me feel as though my body were twisting and spinning instead of relaxing into a good night's rest. Or like in eighth grade, when I took Xanax for the first time, or ninth, when I took Vicodin for period cramps. Yeah. That's what this was like. It was like Vicodin. Totally and completely surreal.

Pretend-me sat there with Amanda, pretending everything was and would be just fine. Real-me was spinning into space.

God help me when the pain kicked back in.

New York, New York

*J*ust like the impulsive man he'd never been, Amanda's dad insisted that the family get out to New York right away. They were leaving on Thursday, five days before my junior year of high school would start. My first year at Whitbread without Amanda. And I still hadn't told her about the divorce. Because if I said it out loud, that would mean I was acknowledging it. And if I did that, I might have to actually believe that it was true. So instead, I kept that secret bottled up inside of me, spinning the problems into a coil that was sure to unwind.

On Thursday morning, Amanda and I sat on her front steps, watching as movers loaded brown cardboard boxes into a truck. She held her knees to her chest and rested her head on my shoulder. We had been best friends for years. I realized then that I didn't have any idea when I might see Amanda next, and suddenly, a short string of words burst from my mouth.

"My parents are getting divorced," I said, watching the clouds above me.

There was silence for a moment, and I lowered my gaze to Amanda's neighbors' house, scared to look Amanda in the eye, thinking maybe I'd spoken so softly and quickly she hadn't heard me. Or maybe I hadn't spoken at all.

"Oh, Becky!" Amanda finally said. "I'm so sorry. When did you find out?"

"Tuesday."

"You know, you could have told me earlier," she said, and she turned away. Her voice was wavering, more hurt than mad.

I hate hurting people. It's something I should be able to control, and yet . . .

I gripped the edge of the brick step that I was sitting on for support. "I know. And I wanted to. But I don't think I really wanted to believe that it was real."

Amanda turned back to me as her dad weaved past us on the front steps and walked down the driveway. He was wearing an "I ♥NY" T-shirt and holding the leash of one of the golden retrievers. "I know exactly what you mean," she said, nodding her head.

We drove over to Larchmont for one last latte together. There were three coffee places on Larchmont: Starbucks, The Coffee Bean & Tea Leaf, and Peet's. Amanda and I always went to Peet's. We had our favorite spot (the armchairs by the front window), and the baristas had memorized our orders. It helped that we always ordered the same thing.

"Two nonfat vanilla lattes and one three-berry scone," I told the girl as Amanda browsed through the magazine collection. We brought our drinks over to the armchairs and sat down.

"I can't believe this is actually happening. I mean, who knows how long it will be before . . . ," I said.

"It's just not fair." Amanda broke a piece off the scone and chewed for a moment, thinking. "My parents only care about what's best for them, not what's best for *me*."

"You're telling me!"

Something caught Amanda's attention and she smiled. I swiveled around to see what it was and saw that it was a *who*.

"Hey." Joey Michaels was smiling down at me. He ran a hand through his shaggy brown hair and nodded to Amanda.

"Hey," I said, gesturing to an empty chair to my left. "Come sit." This conversation had been getting too intense—the situation was becoming too real—and I wanted some breathing room.

Joey and I had been friends since we were little, and through me, Amanda and Joey had become friends as well. It was hard not to like Joey; he was a little goofy and his ears stuck out, but he was also friendly, sincere, and really funny.

"Rarely do I see you here not in uniform," Joey commented, taking a seat.

"Oh, don't worry. I'll be rocking those khaki skirts in

no time," I joked back. I broke off a piece of the scone and held it in my hand.

"But I won't," Amanda added, frowning.

Joey shifted uneasily in his chair. "Yeah, I heard. I'm sorry, Amanda. That sucks." Joey was a Hancock Park kid, too. He went to Whitbread's "brother" school, Stratfield.

"I can't wait for school to start," he said, rolling his eyes. Which was funny because Joey was like me—he probably *was* looking forward to school starting. Why was he pretending to dread it? "I heard that Stratfield's going all out on an environmental campaign this year. They're creating a fucking compost pile next to the soccer field. I bet that'll smell great!"

"Lovely. Oh, and did you hear, they're rebuilding half of Whitbread!" I added.

"Guys, do you know how much it sucks hearing you talk about school when I'm not going to be there to experience any of it?" Amanda put her head in her hands. That was the thing with Amanda—she liked to be in charge of setting the tone of the conversation.

There was a moment of silence. "Sorry," Joey and I said at the same time.

"Thanks."

Joey stood up. "Listen, I should get going. My mom's sick, so I thought I'd come pick up her favorite tea latte for her. Bye, Amanda." Joey leaned in to give her a hug. "Shoot me an e-mail from New York or something. I bet your new school will be great—no construction projects or compost piles, hopefully!" Amanda simply nodded. "And Becky, see you soon." I stood up so he didn't have to lean down to hug me, and I wrapped my arms around him. Cocking his head to whisper in my ear, Joey said, "My mom told me about . . . you know, the divorce. I'm so sorry, Becky. That's really tough. But if you need anything, I'm always here."

As I rested my head against his chest, grateful for the hug, I felt the beginnings of tears in my eyes. "Thanks," I whispered back.

"Are you okay? That was the longest hug ever," Amanda said as I sat back down.

"Yeah." I nodded. "There's just a lot of crap happening in my life, too."

"But at least you're not moving to New York."

I felt a piece of scone get stuck in my throat, and I coughed. "It's not a competition," I said, my voice quiet.

When I drove Amanda back to her house after our coffee trip, there were moving vans in the driveway and along the sidewalk. Boxes were being loaded into the truck, and Amanda's dad was packing suitcases into the car. I parked next to one of the vans and turned to Amanda. "I guess this is it."

"I guess so."

"Call me when you get into New York, okay? And you have to keep me updated on everything that happens."

"Of course. And you'll do the same for me, right? I

don't want to be totally out of the Whitbread loop. You'll have to keep me posted on MUN and, like, what energy drink the Trinity are hooked on this year."

The Trinity was our name for our grade's popular girls. We ridiculed them and envied them at the same time, but we only owned up to the ridicule.

We laughed and hugged, and Amanda got out of the car and started up the front steps. I waved good-bye as if this were just any other day and drove toward home.

Shit Lists

I like to make lists—they help me feel more in control of my life. My lists are always on college-ruled paper and need to have a number of entries that is divisible by three. That night, I sat at my desk and made a Shit List—a list of what parts of my life were awful. I thought that getting it all out on paper would make me feel better, but it didn't. It just made me feel worse. And overwhelmed.

Sara Elder was supposed to be back from her vacation, and the last time I saw her, she promised that she'd be checking voice mail. But I still hadn't received a reply from that emergency phone call two days earlier. A Shit List and my dwindling bottle of Xanax seemed like the best substitute.

The list was detailed. It wasn't good enough to just write *Parents divorcing, best friend moving away, life sucks.* I had to break it down to see what each of these things actually meant. This is what I came up with before I quit:

Home feels empty.
Mom works late.
Dad works later.
Therapist not returning my phone calls.
No real friends at school.
Don't know if I can keep MUN going w/o Amanda.

I looked at the pages spread out before me and started to panic. By that time, I'd taken my last Xanax, and it was too late to get my prescription refilled. So to calm myself down, and for a kind of balance I suddenly, desperately needed, I countered the Shit List with a Bright Side List.

On the bright side: I have all my limbs.
On the bright side: I'm sort of smart (although sometimes I worry I'm not smart enough).
On the bright side: School starts next Tuesday.

I know, that one doesn't seem like a "bright side," but I really was looking forward to digging out my khaki skirts from the box I'd hid them in last June, when I'd been beyond eager to be rid of them for three months. In a few weeks, when I was *thisclose* to burning out because

I'd already overcommitted myself and signed up for one too many classes and ended up with no free periods, I'd probably move the *school* category from the Bright Side List to the Shit List, but right then . . . right then I just hoped that a brand-new spiral notebook could provide some sort of temporary cure. For me, each fresh one is full of promise—that I'll be a diligent note taker, that I might write down brilliant thoughts between those college-ruled lines.

But as I tried to focus on the jolts of excitement this usually sent through me, I came to an unavoidable conclusion: A spiral notebook might not be enough right now. It wouldn't make my parents decide they were just kidding about that whole divorce thing. It wouldn't bring Amanda back. And it definitely wouldn't make me instantly popular at school.

Family Matters

The majority of kids at my school have at least one relative in the Industry (aka Hollywood). I suppose my parents aren't really an exception: Every week on *Kathy's Eye*, my mom advises women on what is "in" and "of the moment." My dad's an entertainment lawyer. He's the guy you call if you're an actor and you want to negotiate a deal for your upcoming movie. Basically, it's a lot of boring paperwork that adds up to invitations to movie premieres and many late nights spent working.

The other thing the kids at my school have at least one of? A stepparent. Because the majority of kids at my school also have divorced parents. Joey's had split up when he was really little, back when I thought divorce was something that could never happen to me.

Suddenly, it seemed like I was becoming a part of the majority in all the wrong ways.

The Friday before school started, my mom and I were supposed to go to brunch at Toast on Third Street. I hadn't really talked to her in days—she'd call and I wouldn't pick up, she'd come in to say good night and I'd pretend to be asleep. And while part of me wanted to keep avoiding her, another part of me needed to hear what she had to say. Dad was barely around at all, so it wasn't hard to avoid him. That morning, when I went down to the kitchen to make my cereal, I ran into him, stumbling in from the adjacent family room, looking as though he hadn't shaved in days. The texture of the pillows from the family room couch was imprinted on Dad's cheek. I had already poured milk into my bowl of Cheerios, but I suddenly felt too sick to eat. I left the room with an awkward "Later" and headed back upstairs.

Mom's show tapes every Friday afternoon, but she says she always has time for me. I felt bad ignoring her—guilty, even. Although I knew that the divorce wasn't my fault and that I had every reason to be upset, I still feared that by avoiding everything, I was making it worse. So I asked Mom if we could go to brunch. She said that she could definitely make time and she'd come by for me at eleven; by noon, I still hadn't heard from her.

I'd spent the morning rewriting my lists so that each fit

on one sheet of paper. At eleven, I'd decided to color code them. By eleven thirty, I had renumbered everything. By noon, I was just pissed and decided to call my mother.

"Hi, honey," Mom said when she answered the phone, as if it were any old day, as if she had nowhere in particular to be.

"Where are you? I thought we were going out to brunch."

"Oh, sweetheart." At least she sounded a little remorseful. "I'm so sorry, I got called in to work early." In the background, I heard a voice asking if my mother might want "an ottoman to go with it."

"An ottoman? Where are you?" I asked again.

She paused for a moment. "I'm furniture shopping. We can't move into an apartment with no furniture in it, can we?"

I gulped and pulled at my shirt, running my fingers along the frayed edges. "Apartment?" Had I missed something? No one had ever mentioned anything about us moving out. In trying to ignore the divorce, I'd blinded myself. Obviously my parents wouldn't want to live together anymore. But although this was obvious, I still was able to avoid acknowledging it.

"Honey, I've found a great place for us. Not for forever, but just for now. It's at the beach. You and Jack will love it, I think. Pam's helped me pick out furniture, and we'll be ready to move in next week. You get your own bathroom, too. No more sharing with Jack."

My own bathroom? Is that what she thought mattered most?

I couldn't think of anything to say to her—nothing appropriate anyway—so I just mumbled, "See you later," and snapped my phone shut without waiting for a response.

My mom was buying furniture for an apartment that I hadn't even known existed. So typical of her! No wonder Dad was divorcing her.

A few minutes later, Dad poked his head into my room. He was dressed for work but had apparently forgotten to brush his hair.

"I'm going to work," he told me.

"Now?" Dad was usually out of the house by eight. Sometimes he left even earlier.

"Um, yeah." He ran a hand through his hair. "I decided to take a nap before going in."

Bullshit. My dad never took naps. What was going on?

"Anyway," Dad continued, "could you see what Jack wants for dinner when he wakes up? And take him to Larchmont and get him some lunch, okay? Maybe sushi? He's having a hard time with this," my dad said.

I sat up on my bed. "*He's* having a hard time? Yes, of course. I'll do absolutely everything I can to make sure his life is wonderful—maybe I'll get him delivery from Spago? What about me, Dad?" My eyes stung, and I stared at the pile of Shit Lists in front of me.

He didn't lean down for the usual hug or kiss, just

stared at me with a confused look on his face. "You're a big girl, Becky," he told me. "I gotta go to work, so . . ."

His words trailed off as if he didn't need to say more, and suddenly everything was clear to me: This was all his fault. If he weren't always at work or on his way to work or late coming home from work, then none of this would be happening!

My mind had flip-flopped quickly, too quickly for me to make sense of anything. But right then he was the one standing in front of me, so he was the one I was blaming.

"I'm so big that I'll move out for good, just like Mom!" I yelled at him.

"Don't be silly," he said, then picked up his briefcase from the floor and walked out of the room, down the stairs, and out the front door.

Blonde Ambition

*I*f there was one thing I hated, it was not having control. But there I was, just sitting back and watching as my life was changing in front of me, and I had no control over what was happening. So I stopped eating. By Saturday, I hadn't really eaten in three days. I liked knowing that I was in charge of what I consumed; nobody else could have that power. That empty feeling proved I could take action, and I wanted the feeling to last and spread. Which is why I decided to accompany my mom to Frédéric Fekkai that morning.

My mom went to Frédéric Fekkai's Rodeo Drive salon every Saturday to get her hair blown out, and every month or so, she'd have her color touched up. Mom was a natural blonde, but she was actually a pretty dark blonde, according to the pictures I'd seen. I'm probably not the best person to ask about my mom's natural hair color, because I've never actually seen it. My hair ended up a sort of middling brown, and I'd been happy enough with it for all my life so far. I didn't get my hair done at Frédéric Fekkai. But nobody turned and stared in horror when I walked by, either.

My mother always told me that I was pretty, but I figured I should take that kind of compliment with a grain of salt. Telling your daughter that she's pretty must be in some sort of rulebook—the Mothers' Code of Conduct. Plus, Mom had repeatedly said that I was just the right size for my height, and I *knew* that wasn't true. Size 8 was way above normal.

For L.A., anyway.

I sat in the passenger seat as my mom drove us to the salon. When we hit a stoplight, Mom turned to me.

"I'm glad you decided to come. This will be fun." She'd been doing this false-cheer thing for a couple days, like, "Look, life is great! What divorce?"

"I hope so." I was feeling guilty about blaming her for the divorce, but I wasn't going to admit that to her. Besides, I couldn't figure out who was actually to blame, my mom or my dad.

"Sweetheart, I know that you're mad at me, and you have every reason to be. I just hope you can understand that if I could have shielded you from this pain, I would have. I love you more than anything in the world."

I wanted to tell her that I loved her, too, but instead I looked down at my hands. The ride was silent after that, and soon we were pulling into the driveway of the hair salon.

The Frédéric Fekkai salon is on Rodeo Drive in Beverly Hills. Fekkai himself is in the Los Angeles salon only one day a month. Getting a haircut from him costs about six hundred dollars.

Which is three times what it costs to feed and educate a child in Africa for a year.

My mom gets her hair colored by Rian and cut by Marcos, and that Saturday, I would, too. I've always liked getting my hair done because no matter how I look when I walk in, I know that I'll look much better when I walk out. I don't really like *being* at this salon, though—all the beautiful women with shiny, layered hair and the clean-cut stylists wielding buzzing blow-dryers makes me feel entirely inadequate and disastrously unattractive. Also, I like to wait as long as I can between haircuts because that maximizes the effect of each one. There's nothing exciting about getting my hair trimmed an eighth of an inch, because I won't look any different. But if I cut off three inches, I could become an entirely different person in a matter of minutes.

Mom greeted the two young receptionists who sat at the circular front desk as though they were old friends, and we continued on to the changing room.

"Two robes, please. Cut and color," Mom said to the older woman who stood behind a window, shelves of towels and robes behind her. The woman took two thin, chocolate-brown robes down from a rack behind her and handed them to my mom.

"Here, put this on," she said, handing me a robe. She took off her sweater and then her shirt and hung them on a wooden hanger.

"Do I need to take off my . . ." My voice cut short. I looked down at myself. I was wearing a turquoise tank top and jean shorts. The receptionists were wearing crisp, white button-downs and black pants, and the woman I'd seen perusing the makeup at the counters behind the receptionist desk was wearing head-to-toe Chanel. I hadn't known that I was supposed to dress up to go to the hair salon. Even my mom, although not in designer attire, looked totally polished.

She looked at me, really looked at me, for the first time in days, and smiled. "You can just put the robe on over your clothes."

We headed to the salon floor, where scissors clicked and the hum of blow-dryers overpowered everything else. And, of course, there were mirrors everywhere. Further back, we entered a smaller room; the hairstylists there wore cream-colored shirts instead of white ones. This, my mom explained, was the room where color was done. Mom gestured for me to sit down in one of the dark brown leather chairs, but I paused a moment, staring at myself in the mirror, standing behind the chair. Rian, a tall, thin woman with bobbed blonde hair, darted over to us, and I self-consciously tugged the tie on my robe a little tighter. I hate robes like this because they generally make me feel short and stumpy.

"So nice to meet you," Rian said, running her hands through my hair. "You've got a gorgeous base color. Are you thinking of going lighter? Doing highlights?"

"Um, thanks," I said. Base color? Was that a compliment? Or was that like saying this is a good starting place—a good canvas. Was I just a good blank page?

"Yeah, highlights, I guess. I want something different. Something new." I looked at my mom.

"Do whatever you want," Mom said. "I just want you to be happy."

I looked back up at the mirror. Rian was staring back at me, and I looked deep into her eyes. Clichés flew at me. Brunettes do it better. Blondes have more fun. And redheads? Well, I wouldn't work as a redhead anyway.

Brunettes do it better. Yeah, maybe that's true. But maybe doing everything better isn't such a good thing. Blondes have more fun. It's possible; who knows? I knew that I certainly didn't have that much fun. I sighed and swiveled my chair around to face Rian, who was chatting animatedly with my mom about a recent episode of *Kathy's Eye*.

"I want to go lighter," I said. "Much lighter."

And two hours later, I loosened the ties of my robe and walked out into the Beverly Hills sunlight, a brand-new blonde.

Uniformity

The conventional wisdom about a school like Whitbread is that it must be *so great* to go to an all-girls' school that has a uniform, because it means we can just roll out of bed in the morning, put on a skirt, and head to school without having to worry about what we look like.

Yeah—not exactly. Two types of girls attend Whitbread: There are the girls who do just roll out of bed in the morning and head off to school, and then there are the "flair" girls—girls who accessorize their uniforms as much as they can possibly get away with.

For me, getting dressed for school is a process, not a roll-out-of-bed kind of thing. But not because I'm a flair girl, more because I'm . . . particular. For example, if I'm wearing the white collared shirt, I refuse to wear the white sweater. If I'm wearing the navy blue collared shirt, I can't wear the navy sweater. My socks have to rise to no more than one inch above my sneakers, and my skirt can't have wrinkles.

I always set out my clothes the night before the first day of school, and my backpack is always prepacked. But this year, I decided to wait until the day-of to pick my outfit. I think it was my attempt to be just a little bit more like everyone else.

But as I dug through my closet Tuesday morning trying to find a navy blue shirt that would work with my white sweater, waiting until the last minute didn't seem like such a bright idea.

Finally settling on a button-up cardigan, I zipped my backpack, put my phone on vibrate and tucked it into the pocket of my skirt (which was hanging on my hips instead of my waist—another perk of not eating), and headed down the stairs. Today was the first day that I was allowed to drive to school. Only juniors and seniors are allowed to drive to school because the parking lot isn't big enough. Of course, the upcoming renovation would leave us with a couple floors of underground parking, so future sophomores wouldn't be forced to wait like I was. I didn't live far away from school. So I didn't *really* need to drive. But it was the principle that mattered. That and my thirty-pound backpack. Mostly, I wanted to start off this year differently—with a bang. And not the kind of bang that came from huffing and puffing under the weight of my backpack, walking into school with my face red and my skirt riding up.

I didn't need to be at school until eight, but I was ready to leave at seven-thirty. Grabbing my car keys off of the front hall table, to the silent house I shouted, "Good-bye." Stratfield had one more week of summer break, so Jack was still asleep. I had no idea where my parents were.

I drove down Third Street, passing the Wilshire Country Club golf course and that mansion with the naked statues in the front yard. After a few blocks, the big white building that is Whitbread came into view. To enter the parking lot, I had to drive past the ivy-covered front entrance and turn left in the middle of the block. The car waiting in front of me for the parking lot was an Audi, and the car that turned in behind me was a Prius. Priuses and Audis were among the most popular cars at school, although there were quite a few Mercedes and BMWs as well. The Audi was struggling to pull into a tight spot, and the security guard was gesturing wildly, trying to help the girl. I pulled around her and parked in an empty spot in the back of the lot, just behind a light blue convertible. Leaving my keys in the car, I stepped out into the pleasantly warm air. If you parked in the lot, you had to leave your keys, just in case one of the security guards had to move your car to let out another car. It's all a part of the Whitbread Honor Code.

You wear the uniform, you adhere to the Code.

The Horny Trinity

*I*t was early still, but the campus had already begun to fill up with students. I walked up the steps, past senior girls who were writing in lipstick on the faces of underclassmen their class year. I set down my backpack along a wall near the library. At Whitbread, we're allowed to put down our belongings anywhere on campus and come back to pick them up later. Nobody ever steals anything. As I started down the north hallway, I passed two girls with large sunglasses, messy hair, and skirts rolled over so short that most of their boxer shorts were showing. One of them lowered her sunglasses and gave me a once-over. Alissa Hargrove. The head of the Trinity.

Amanda and I had anointed them the Horny Trinity in

the ninth grade after we heard about some sex toy party Alissa had hosted. That we weren't invited to, of course.

Alissa readjusted the large designer bag she had hoisted over her shoulder. The bag must have weighed at least as much as she did. I had this theory that Alissa Hargrove didn't actually eat (like, for real—not for few-day stints, which was all I could manage), and I had yet to see anything that would disprove it. Also, for the past year or so, there had been a rumor going around that she did coke. Which, I guess, would help with the staying-skinny thing. Her long, gray cashmere sweater vest hung loosely over her nonexistent hips. She, naturally, was one of the "flair" girls. Gray wasn't actually in uniform, but somehow she managed to get away with wearing it. I smiled pleasantly and said, "Hey."

Alissa paused for a moment, then nodded. "Hey." We'd been going to school together for twelve years—since kindergarten at our progressive private elementary school—but she looked at me as if she'd have to think *really* hard to come up with my name. I thought about Barneys and her dad's hand on my back and blushed a little.

Courtney Gross, the girl with Alissa, gave me a shy smile. I had never had a full conversation with her, but she seemed nice enough. Instead of a collared shirt, she was wearing a white tank top with a rhinestone frog on the chest. My mom had featured that brand on her show— the company custom-designed these shirts, which cost a fortune. I was just about to ask the generic first-day-of-school question—"How was your summer?"—but I was stopped by an overexcited Kimberly Turner. "Guys," she squealed to Alissa and Courtney, "the new Junior Living Room is fab! They installed a refrigerator and TV in there for us." The three of them were essentially the most popular girls in my grade, and I felt awkward, standing there on the edge of their conversation. I was about to make an excuse to keep on walking when Kim turned to me. "Omigod, Becky, how was your summer?"

Kim is tall and gesticulates a lot when she speaks. She always reminds me of her mother; the energy never fades. We used to be friendly because her mom always brought her to the Hollywood Women's Political Committee meetings at my house. Her mom was a dedicated member of the group, but Kim stopped coming to HWPC meetings once she became cool and had better friends to hang out with. Kim and I had also gone to elementary school together, but even with being thrown together because of our moms, we hadn't ever been *friends.*

"My summer was really good," I replied. *It would be really nice,* I thought, *if her mom hadn't told her about my parents getting divorced.* Because if she had, not only would the whole grade know about it, but also my "I had a great summer" disguise would be ruined. "How was yours?"

"Ah-mazing. Did you lose weight? You look awesome. I lost weight. I lost two pounds. P.S.—I love the blonde. It's fab on you. So, I should get to Advisory," Kim said, all in one breath. "Do you want a Red Bull? I have, like, a six-pack in here, and I brought a carton for the Junior Living Room. You know, first day of school pick-me-up, whatever." She shrugged her shoulders and nodded her head rapidly. I wondered how many Red Bulls she'd already had. I thought about mentioning that the "bull" in Red Bull is because of the taurine that's in it, which was originally found in bull bile, but I thought better of it. Facts like that weren't exactly friend-winning.

"Sure." I choked back a momentary repulsion and the fear that if Amanda could see me, she wouldn't approve, and I grabbed a can from her bag. "Thanks. I should get going, but good to see you," I said, and I awkwardly continued down the hall, thinking about how that was the longest conversation Kim and I had had in years.

School Daze

*S*eventh graders rushed ahead of me, dragging their rolling backpacks behind them, desperate to be on time to class on the first day. As a student advisor, I would get to know some of these girls throughout the year, but I had no idea who my co-advisor would be now that Amanda was gone. Whitbread had a student advising system that paired two juniors or seniors with one faculty member and ten underclassmen. Not every junior or senior did it—but I was the type who did. The idea was that we, the student advisors, would help the younger girls navigate the rocky waters of adolescence and Whitbread. Because we were so much older and wiser.

I reached Mr. Elwright's classroom, took a deep breath,

and opened the door. Inside were ten seventh graders, twenty backpacks, and several tote bags filled with brand-new binders and colored pencils. I spotted Mr. Elwright struggling with the printer. When he saw me, he waded through the mess of school supplies to greet me. "How was your summer?" he asked. Then, before I could answer he turned to the seventh graders and said, "Girls, why is all of this in my room?"

"Is there somewhere else we can put it?" a girl whose skirt went down past her knees asked.

"Yeah, anywhere!" Mr. Elwright exclaimed, moving a plastic bag of locker shelves so that he could reach his coffee.

"Mr. Elwright." I nudged him. "It's their first day. They don't know about the purple lines." Mr. Elwright had never dealt with seventh graders before. He was the MUN advisor, and he usually taught only in the upper school. And there was a reason for that: He wasn't one for patience.

"You can leave your stuff mostly anywhere around campus," I explained to the new girls.

The door opened from behind me, and a heavy bag hit me in the calves. "Oops, sorry. Hey." Taylor Tremaine, the only girl in my class who still occasionally wore her waist-length hair in pigtails, entered the room. "So you're my co-advisor?" she asked, nodding toward me and stating the obvious.

I popped the top of Kim's Red Bull and took a long gulp as I sat down on top of a nearby desk. "Yeah." This wasn't exactly who I had had in mind for a co-advisor. It totally sucked that Amanda couldn't be here, but I had sort of been hoping that this might be an opportunity to get to know someone cool. That is, cooler than me. And definitely cooler than Taylor.

"I was so glad I got to do this. I mean, I only found out last week that they had an opening. Because . . ." She stopped. "Sorry. I mean, I'm sorry Amanda left. It's just . . . I hope we'll have a good year, right?"

"Yeah," I said again, trying to smile my most enthusiastic smile. I looked out at our charges, who were busy comparing their schedules for the day. Taylor was probably a nice girl. I shouldn't be so quick to judge. It was just that . . . well, she still occasionally brought a rolling backpack to school. Even I knew better than to do that. I wondered when I had most recently spoken with Taylor. I mean, she did drama. That was a world away from Model UN. I couldn't even remember if she had been in any of my classes last year.

Advisory was seven minutes long. Exactly. It began at 7:50 and ended at 7:57—Whitbread had an odd way of timing classes. As Taylor explained important first-day information and answered questions from the seventh graders, Mr. Elwright pulled me aside. "Becky," he said, straightening his polka-dotted tie. Mr. Elwright was famous for wearing suits, even on casual-dress Fridays. "How are you doing? Is everything going okay, you know, without Amanda?"

"I'm doing fine," I said, with a harsher tone than I intended. "I mean, I don't *need* Amanda. . . ." Really, I was scared that I did need her. But I didn't want to admit that.

The bell rang, and I turned to leave. "Wait," Mr. Elwright said, reaching out and putting a hand on my shoulder. I turned back to face him. "We need to meet about MUN."

"Okay." I nodded. "My schedule's outside. I can e-mail you with my free periods."

"That sounds good. Listen, Becky, everyone loved what you did last year, with Pakistan and coming up with the activism component." I nodded again, staring at the map on the wall behind Mr. Elwright. His face grew softer, and he lowered his voice a little. "You know, you can do this, even without Amanda. You've been leading this club all along." He paused, and although I wasn't looking directly at him, I could feel his eyes on me.

"Yeah," I replied. "Thanks."

"I mean it, Becky. You'll survive this. And you'll be wonderful at leading this club." The start-of-class bell rang. Mr. Elwright looked down at his desk and shuffled a few papers; I shifted my feet a little, wondering whether I should go. "Okay, that's it for my motivational speech. Go to class. Don't be late." He reached over his desk and patted me awkwardly on the shoulder.

"Have a good first day," I called as I walked out the door.

* * *

First period that day was an All-School Assembly across campus in the Whitbread Auditorium. The whole school, faculty included, fit into that one room, where the seating sections were assigned by grade. I started to walk toward the sophomore entrance but quickly corrected myself, instead heading down the hallway to the back of the auditorium. The noise of squealing seventh graders mixed with the sound of reuniting upper schoolers (the all-girls alternative to upperclass*men*), and at the front of the room, a projector screen was being set up. There was an empty seat next to Taylor Tremaine, and despite the fact that I wasn't sure I liked her—and that hanging out with her certainly wouldn't increase my social prospects—I urged myself to go sit next to her. It's not like I had a lot of other options. "Hey," I said, sitting down. "Do you know what this year's assembly is about?"

"The construction project, probably."

I nodded. "I heard it was going to last three years. Sucks we won't get to be here for the result."

"Yeah, but I'm kind of ready to get out of here. Aren't you? This place is like a bubble."

At that moment, as if on cue, Kim Turner, who was seated in the row in front of us and had been craning her neck to scan the room, spotted me and stopped. "Oh, Becky, I forgot to say this earlier . . . but I'm so sorry about your parents!"

I grimaced. Thanks, Whitbread bubble.

Up at the podium, Ms. Morton, our head of school, cleared her throat into the microphone. "Welcome back, girls. I hope you've all had a wonderful summer. I am very excited to share with you the details of our new construction project!"

Whitbread had recently decided that our state-of-the-art art studios weren't state-of-the-art enough, and that we could use a bigger, better library. Plus the underground parking.

It's a sixty-five-million-dollar project.

Taylor and I looked at each other, each with raised eyebrows. It struck me that maybe Taylor was different from the other Hollywoodified robots in my grade. And maybe that was a good thing. But was she *too* different?

The lights dimmed, and a slideshow revealed what our new ceramics studio and photography darkroom would look like, along with a large student resource center filled with couches and computers and a cafeteria. Photographs of current Whitbread students had been Photoshopped into the slideshow, as if to prove just how great this would be for future Whitbread students. At the end of the slideshow, about half of the students cheered, and a couple of teachers rolled a tented table to the front of the stage.

"Now, in honor of the new construction, and to thank you all for supporting and enduring it, we have a few goodies for you. Coming around are pins for our new Construction Campaign, and here"—Ms. Morton paused as she walked toward the table that had just been wheeled out—"is something I think you'll all like." She pulled off the tented cloth. I couldn't see the stage very well, so I missed the big reveal. "Girls, this is a model of what the school will look like after the construction. And here's the great part—it's a cake!"

There were gasps and murmurs in the audience. "Is she kidding?" I whispered to Taylor. "A cake model of the school? Isn't that a little excessive?"

Taylor shrugged. "Of course it's excessive. It's Whitbread."

Warning Signs

*A*s soon as I got home from school, I laid out my calculus homework in front of me on my bed. I meant to actually do the homework, but I guess at some point I must have fallen asleep, because two hours later, my cheek was pressed against my open textbook, and my mom was calling my name. Groggily, I sat up on my bed. Mom had come in and sat down at the edge. "How was school?" she asked.

"I . . . it was . . ." I shrugged. I usually shared all the details of my life with her, so this avoiding-her business was hard. But if I suddenly started talking to her again, she might think that I was giving in—that I wasn't really mad at her for this whole divorce thing.

I guess my mom read my mind. "Honey," she said,

"you must have known this was coming. The divorce. All the warning signs were there."

I folded my arms tightly across my chest. If this was her way of comforting me, it was a lousy one. As my mom waited for me to say something, one particular memory stuck out in my mind. It had been a few months earlier, on a Friday night. We were all sitting down at the table—Mom, Dad, Jack, and I—when we realized that nobody had made dinner. Usually, Mom cooked or we went out, but once in a while, Dad made dinner. Dad was a better cook than Mom, who often got distracted and forgot ingredients. I wasn't sure if that Friday was meant to be my mom's or my dad's night to cook, and apparently I wasn't the only one who couldn't remember. The silence was painful as we sat at the table behind empty plates.

Mom and Dad excused themselves to the kitchen, but the walls are thin, and Jack and I could hear their conversation clearly.

"Kathy, ever since this show started . . . ," Dad had begun.

"Harold, this has nothing to do with my show. Besides, I'm doing something I love; you should be happy for me."

"It's not that I'm not happy for you, it's just that this is disrupting things. You're less available for the kids . . . and for me."

"Less available? Me?" My mom's voice got higher and louder practically with each word. "Harold, I do my research from home. My political committee meetings are held here. I am always available when the kids—or you—need me. It's not me who's unavailable, it's you! You're so disengaged, you don't even realize how much you're working. This is projection—that's what my shrink calls it—projection, Harold!"

The conversation had gone on, but either I'd stopped listening or I'd blocked the memory of it out of my mind, because I can't remember what had happened next.

Maybe I *had* seen it coming. Maybe I just didn't want to admit that it was true. Thinking back on that dinner, I found myself growing angry with my dad—the way he had acted really wasn't fair to my mom.

"I rented that apartment I was telling you about," Mom said when it was clear I wasn't going to break my silence. "We're going to move next week, sweetie. Your father and I have decided that you and Jack will split your time between us, half and half. No lawyers or anything, so that's good, right? One week with him, and one with me. That seems fair, right?"

I looked away. She wasn't really asking my opinion, after all.

"Sweetheart, please. I could use some help here." When I still didn't respond, she put a hand on my shoulder. I shrugged it away. "This whole situation is pretty tough on me, you know?"

"Tough on you? What about me, Mom? What about *me*?"

She didn't say anything. I knew that she was right—of

course she was right, *her* life was about to change, too—but that didn't matter to me right then. That wasn't my problem; it was hers. "Not only are my parents getting divorced, but I found out through a slip-of-the-tongue by my psycho grandmother. And I'm almost out of tranquilizers, and Sara Elder hasn't answered any of my calls, and my best friend just moved away!"

Mom looked hurt, but her eyes softened. "I'll call Sara Elder in the morning," she said. "And I can't even express how sorry I am about Grandma. As for Amanda, I'm sure she'll be back in no time. You've met her parents—you think they'll survive one New York winter?" I knew she was trying to make a joke, but nothing seemed funny in that moment. "Besides, look on the bright side: Now you'll have a chance to make new friends. Plus, you have Joey."

It was true; I did have Joey. But unless I put him in a skirt and gave him a wig, he was no help when it came to the problem of who I was going to sit with at lunch.

"I'm so sorry, sweetheart, but can you understand a little bit where I'm coming from with this?"

I shook my head no, not knowing exactly what she meant.

"It's not like I just woke up one day and thought it would be a good idea to get a divorce. This has been building for a while. And moving out—well, it's a good way for me to get a fresh start. I can't stay here. This is your father's house."

It was weird to hear her say that. I'd always thought of this as *our* house. Not his or hers.

"It's hard, being here," she went on, "you know, when your dad is never home. And even when he is here . . . well, he's not *really* here." And then she started talking about the lump she'd found in her breast a few years ago, which seemed like a non sequitur to me.

My stomach aching, I turned away once again and found myself stuck facing a large mirror that was mounted on the wall next to one of my bookcases. Staring, I tried to focus on the reflection of the girl looking back at me: bright blonde hair and flat brown eyes, the residue of eyeliner from several days ago creating shadows beneath them. Was this really me? Behind me was the reflection of my mom, still in work clothes, her head resting on one of her fists, eyes glassy. I had her eyes and her nose. And when we smiled, people said that I had her smile. But neither of us was smiling now. I remembered how I had always wanted to be just like her, back when I was little and she was perfect.

"You stayed at Amanda's that day, so you wouldn't remember. But your dad didn't even offer to come to the hospital with me. I took a taxi," Mom said, pulling at the fraying edges of my duvet cover.

I was in the eighth grade when my mom had a breast cancer scare. She was so frightened. I was, too. How could my dad have done that? It couldn't have been *my* dad—the Dad who used to take me out to get pancakes for dinner, who would pretend to be a horse so that I could ride on his back around and around the bedroom. Was it possible? Then I realized it was definitely possible, since I hadn't exactly seen that Dad in a long time.

I turned back to face Mom. "I'd never make you take a taxi to the hospital," I told her as I reached into her arms, hot tears dripping down my cheeks.

Current Affairs

*T*here are certain perks for juniors at Whitbread that sophomores just don't have. Like, juniors can go off campus for lunch or leave early if they have free periods at the end of the day. But best of all, juniors have their own designated living room. (Seniors do, too, but ours is just as good as theirs.) Couches and armchairs line the walls, and pastel-colored beanbag chairs—for that special teenage feel, I guess—are planted throughout, with some grouped around an oak coffee table. The Living Room, which most people just refer to as the Room, is where all of us juniors hang out during our free periods. Most girls bring their laptops to school and spend hours analyzing photos from recent premieres and cocktail parties (the entire campus has WiFi, of course). A whiteboard, which hangs on one of the walls, sometimes gets used to tally up who in the grade had garnered the most mentions on gossip websites over the weekend—whether for wearing a one-of-a-kind designer dress to an exclusive party or flipping off one of the paparazzi. The winner was usually Alissa Hargrove.

I was beginning to warm up to Taylor. She was nice, albeit eccentric with an occasional unwanted attention-drawing laugh. And despite the fact that I knew she wasn't going to help me win popular friends, I preferred sitting with Taylor in the Room to sitting alone. I didn't want to seem *absolutely* friendless. She had a group of drama friends, and they were all . . . nice. But I had even less in common with her friends than I did with her. Taylor wasn't in the Room all the time, though—she did have to go to class, after all. And sitting alone on a couch with a schoolbook in my lap, anxiously watching everyone else socialize and wondering how I might convince the Trinity to nod my way, was not good for my mental state. So sometimes, I hid in Mr. Elwright's classroom, doing research for Model UN.

"Just couldn't tear yourself away from world events for one whole day, could you?" Mr. E. asked me once when I plopped my backpack down on a desk and sat behind it. I was back in his classroom for the second time that day.

"No, I couldn't," I volleyed back. "I was sitting in English class, wondering what Uganda's gross domestic product is. I just had to come and look it up!"

"Oh—speaking of, I received our country assignment for this year." Mr. E. stood up and began to dig through piles of papers on his desk. In terms of organization, Mr. E. was the anti-me. After a few minutes, he held up a piece of paper, triumphant. "So it's a good thing that you're finding out Uganda's gross domestic product."

"We have Uganda?" I asked, excited.

"Yep."

"That's great!" I half squealed. "There are plenty of schools that need building in Uganda."

"That's for sure," Mr. E. said, sitting back down. "One more thing: The Parents Association wants you to speak about MUN at their next meeting. You worked so hard last year, and they thought you'd be perfect at getting kids excited about the program."

I smiled, secretly flushing up with pride. Somebody had noticed. Somebody had realized how hard I worked.

The bell rang.

"Shit, I have bio," I said and then looked sheepishly at Mr. Elwright.

He was chuckling. "Language," he said. Then, "Hey, what is Uganda's gross domestic product, anyway?"

Even though I knew he was joking, I rattled off the answer, then headed on to biology.

State of the Union

$\mathcal{S}$ara Elder had finally called back. I wasn't home when she called—which kind of sucked because I had been practicing what I was going to say to her—so my mom talked to her. Mom told me about it over a dinner of cereal and fruit salad. It was just Mom, Jack, and me. I didn't know where Dad was, and I didn't especially want to ask.

"So I made you an appointment for Monday afternoon. Is that okay? I just wanted to take advantage of the fact that I had her on the phone."

"Whatever."

"Mom, can I have the milk?" Jack asked.

"Sure." Mom reached for the milk, and as she passed it

to Jack, she said, "We're moving on Monday."

"Fabulous. Sounds like Monday's going to be a *great* day." I spoke with as much sarcasm as I could muster. I jabbed my fork into a grape.

"Honey, please. I know you're upset, but I'm doing the best I can." She turned to Jack and said, "Remember, you start school next Tuesday."

"Shit! Are you fucking serious?"

"You don't curse like that at school, do you?" my mom asked.

Jack shrugged.

"What would dinner be without some attractive swear words, courtesy of Jack?" I said, loving the protection that sarcasm provided me.

"Exactly!" Jack agreed, uncapping the milk and pouring it over his bowl of Frosted Flakes. "And what would dinner be without the creative Miller cuisine?"

So it was our last week of living as a four-person family. It wasn't that I thought things were so great for the four of us, but I was scared of what changes the move would bring. Especially since we all walked on a tightrope of mental health. One gust of wind and we might trip, might find ourselves dangling, our hands slipping, struggling to hold on.

Dad wasn't shaving and maybe wasn't sleeping either. I came downstairs one morning and stumbled into the kitchen to get an apple and a Diet Coke. Dad was standing at the kitchen counter in the dark, an empty coffee cup in front of him.

"Hello?" I took a step forward and flipped on the light switch. "Are you okay?"

"Becky! Oh, um, yeah." Dad turned to face me. He wore a wrinkled white button-down, with his tie loosened around his neck, and an old pair of sweatpants. "You heading to school soon?" he asked, rubbing the stubble on his cheek.

"Yeah." I nodded, waiting for more, wanting more. Dad and I hadn't discussed the divorce. It was just lurking in the room, sucking up all the air and conversation. We didn't talk about the divorce; we didn't really talk at all. Dad had never been one for confronting emotional situations. I took an apple from the refrigerator, and my dad reached for the jar of instant coffee crystals. "Have a good day," I told him.

"You, too, sweetheart."

Maybe we were dangling already.

Sara Elder, or the Remainders

I'd been seeing Sara Elder since I was in the fifth grade. One day, I came home from school and told my parents that I felt bad for the numbers in long division problems. "What numbers?" they asked me.

"The remainders," I told them. "The ones that get left over. The ones nobody wants. So I'm remembering them, making sure they know someone cares about them."

Mom had leaned forward, her head on her fist, and asked me to explain. Dad had just sort of sat there, shifting his leg nervously. I listed out the remainders of the fifty long division problems that I had done that day. I had started storing those numbers in my head, and once I started, I couldn't seem to stop. Apparently, this wasn't normal, so my mom asked her psychiatrist for a recommendation, and a phone call was made to Sara Elder.

I spent a year, from fifth grade to sixth grade, sitting in Sara Elder's office for an hour each week, oftentimes refusing to talk to her at all, upset that my parents had forced me into therapy in the first place. It wasn't until the end of sixth grade, when I was obsessively organizing my bookshelves every weekend—alternating between arranging the books by genre, author, and title—that I thought maybe talking to Sara Elder could help. It occurred to me that she wouldn't have any idea how to help me unless I talked to her and told her what I wanted help with. She may have been a doctor who worked with the mind, but that didn't mean that she could read it.

Jack one-upped me for his Get Into Therapy card. (He sees a different psychiatrist than I do, of course, in order to provide us with our necessary "personal space.") He started in the fifth grade, too, so by the time of the divorce he'd been going for only about two years. His act of insanity was pretty brilliant. In response to the school bully and Jack's personal tormentor, August Cartwright, calling him a Jew and making it clear that it was the worst thing a ten-year-old boy could be, Jack hacked into his elementary school computer system and set up a web site that portrayed August as a Nazi in full Heil Hitler mode.

Jack's private elementary school was concerned and definitely not pleased. Neither were my parents, although they were certainly impressed with Jack's Web design skills.

Jagged Little Pill

I woke up on Monday morning, said good-bye to my mom and to my dad, and went to school. I could almost pretend that everything was normal, but I couldn't avoid the inevitable. Because just a few hours later, my mom and dad would no longer be living in one house.

And neither would I.

I was surprised at myself. I had anticipated being upset, but instead I felt numb. I spent all of last-period English staring at my watch, willing the seconds to pass more quickly—not because I couldn't wait to get out of school, see Sara Elder, and go to my mom's new apartment—but because I just wanted to get it all over with.

After school, I drove to Westwood to Sara Elder's office.

A bag in my trunk held pajamas, an extra uniform, jeans, a sweatshirt, and my medications. It was almost as though I were going to a friend's house to sleep over—except not. I had directions to the new apartment, and after I finished with Sara Elder, I was supposed to head over there.

My appointment was for four o'clock, and after years of making this drive, I knew exactly how much time I had to allot, how long it would take to park, and which elevator was the slowest.

Sara Elder worked on the seventh floor of a bland office building in Westwood, and her waiting room was devastatingly boring. It resembled a cramped and entirely beige living room. Over the course of six years, her taste in magazines hadn't changed or developed, and she never threw a single issue away. Copies of *Better Homes & Gardens* and *Good Housekeeping* from 2003 were stacked in piles on the coffee table. For a psychiatrist who specialized in children, she seemed to have very little knowledge about what kids my age might want to read while they waited.

I flicked the switch that would announce my arrival and sat down on the couch, fuming and ready to confront my MIA psychiatrist. A few minutes later, she opened the heavy oak door that led to her office, and I felt the anger rise within me.

"Hello," she said, welcoming me as if nothing were wrong, as if she hadn't completely ignored my *emergency* call. Despite the heat outside, she was wearing a bright red sweater set. "How are you?" she asked once we were both sitting down.

I didn't answer. What kind of question was that? I stared past Sara Elder, past her hair and her gaze, to the orange tapestry with the heart in the center, hanging on the wall behind her. I tried to see if I could count the stitches from where I was sitting.

"Becky?" she leaned forward.

I leaned back. "I called your emergency line. *Emergency.* You didn't call me back for two days. My life is doing a belly flop into who the hell knows where, and you're supposed to be there for me. Thanks for nothing." I surprised myself with the fury that rushed out of me. My breathing came in faster bursts, and my eyes stung.

"Becky, is this really about you being angry with me?"

I wanted to scream, "Don't give me that psychobabble bullshit!" But instead I just sat there, seething.

Sara Elder went on, talking about how this wasn't the end of the world, and I had to concentrate on me, and I don't really know what else she was saying because I, admittedly, wasn't giving her my full attention.

Then, toward the end of the session, she asked, "How are your meds? You seem a little on edge."

Thanks to Sara Elder, I basically had a pharmacy in my bathroom. Everything but the ADD stuff. I'd never had a problem with paying attention. Unfortunately. Just the opposite. I tapped my feet, one then the other and back again, and clenched my hands, one, two, three. I had to do things in multiples of three. "No, I'm doing wonderfully, thanks for asking," I responded, coating my words with sarcasm.

"Why don't we up the Topamax by half a milligram? That ought to help even out your moods a little bit. I'll call the prescription into Rite Aid, okay?"

I nodded and stood up to leave. "Okay. Bye."

I walked out into the hallway, still disappointed in myself that I hadn't fully expressed my rage, and that she hadn't responded to it at all. But at least I was getting more Topamax. Maybe that would calm me down.

I hadn't always been this open, or even open at all, to the idea of medication. The idea that a pill could control my moods, my instincts, and what went on in my mind used to be terrifying. Topamax was my first prescription, and the only one I'd consistently stuck with. The dose, however, had increased steadily throughout the years. I remember the terror, standing in front of the pharmacy counter at Rite Aid, waiting for the pharmacist to fill my first prescription. Mom was next to me, credit card in hand, waiting to pay. I stuffed the little white paper bag into my backpack, nervous that I might run into someone I knew, and that they might wonder why I had a bag from the pharmacy.

That night, after I had brushed my teeth, washed my face, and changed into my pajamas, I went into the bathroom and placed the bright orange medicine bottle on the counter in front of me. "You're going to take half a pill tonight, okay? Just half a pill each day," I remembered

Sara Elder saying. Carefully uncapping the bottle, I stared down at the round, white pills. I had never swallowed a pill before. When I got sick, my parents still bought the chewable or drinkable versions of medicine. At that time, Jack and I still shared a bottle of gummy vitamins. What if—what if this pill got stuck in my throat, and I couldn't figure out how to swallow it? And if I did manage to swallow it without choking, it was going to change the way my brain functioned?!

Skip GO and collect two hundred bucks—I was officially freaked out.

As carefully as I could, I removed one pill from the bottle. It was small and felt chalky between my fingertips. Sara Elder had said to break it in half, and it had sounded easy then, but once I was home I wasn't so sure. There were no dotted lines on the pill, no directions on the bottle; how would I be able to tell if I had successfully broken the little white pill into equal halves? And what if I swallowed two-thirds of the pill by mistake? I could only assume that two-thirds of the pill would affect me more than one half would, and I didn't necessarily want that extra kick right away.

The problems were endless. I gripped the pill and ran down the hall toward my parents' bedroom. "Mom, I don't know how to do this! How am I going to get the pill into two equal parts?" I was becoming hysterical. I walked past her, into their bathroom, calling back to her as I walked.

She was sitting at her computer. "Just break it in half. Hold both ends and pull it apart. Don't worry, you'll get it close enough."

I grasped the pill between my thumb and forefinger and, holding my breath, I pulled apart. I had a piece of the pill in each hand, and I was afraid at first because chalky dust was falling from the pill's jagged edges onto the granite countertop. "Did you get it? Just put it in your mouth and swallow now. Take a deep breath and swallow," Mom called over from her desk. There was a glass of water next to me on the granite countertop. I looked at my reflection in the mirror and shook my head.

"I can't do it, Mom!" I yelled out into the bedroom.

"Becky, I have to finish writing this article! Just swallow it; it's a little pill. Do you know how many pills I have to take every day?"

I looked toward my mom's sink. To the right of it, there was a tray filled with little orange bottles.

Just swallow, just swallow, I told myself, looking at the half pill in my left hand. One deep breath, one big gulp, one little pill. Just swallow.

And with one deep breath and one big gulp, I swallowed that one little pill. And then waited for the magic to happen.

Home Sweet Home?

*I*n twenty minutes, I had gone from the office buildings of Westwood to the apartment buildings of Santa Monica. But it felt like I was on a different planet.

Driving home from my appointment with Sara Elder that day, I almost turned the wrong way on Wilshire—toward my dad's house. Grimacing, I corrected myself and turned right instead of left. I didn't typically spend much time in Santa Monica. Once in a while, I would go to the beach or to the Third Street Promenade, but that was basically it. It seemed that now, I would be learning to call Santa Monica "home."

I double-checked the address before pulling into a tall, cream-colored building on Ocean Avenue, the last street before the water. I stopped in the middle of the large, circular driveway, and a valet in a dark blue uniform came over to open my door. "Is this Beach Tower?" I asked, skeptical. This seemed more like a hotel than an apartment building.

The valet—PEDRO, his name tag said—nodded. He took my keys and began to get into my car.

"Wait!" I said. "There's stuff I need in the trunk."

Another valet appeared, carting a dolly full of groceries. "Oh, don't worry, we'll bring it up for you. What apartment number?"

"Um, 903?"

"We'll be just a few minutes."

Yet another valet held open the glass door that led to the lobby, and I entered tentatively. The lobby was heavily air-conditioned, and the ceilings were high and arched. My sneakers squeaked against the marble floor, and a large mirror hung on the wall opposite the glass entrance, framed by large, multicolored orchids. I didn't see any elevators, so I went over to the concierge desk, which was built into the left wall. "Excuse me," I said. Then, when I had caught the attention of the tall, thin man who stood behind the desk, I added, "Where are the elevators?" The man looked me up and down, and I felt instantly self-conscious about the wrinkle in my uniform skirt and the childish backpack on my back.

"Are you a visitor?" he asked.

"No. I, uh, I live here." The words felt strange. "My

mom just moved in, I mean."

"Miller?" He asked. I nodded. "You must be . . . Rebecca," he said, scanning a list of names.

"Yeah. Becky."

"Nice to meet you. My name is George, and if there's anything I can assist you with, please let me know."

"Could you tell me where the elevators are?" I repeated.

He nodded. "Yes, but I'll need to take you because you don't have your passkey yet. Here, follow me."

I had never been inside an elevator that I couldn't work on my own. This was a hotel, not a home. George nodded toward a colleague at the concierge desk. As if on cue, an elevator opened. Freaky? Apparently not. "The elevators open with permission from the concierge," explained George, "and therefore, nobody who shouldn't be in the building makes it past the lobby."

I nodded because I didn't know what else to do.

"But then, once you get in the elevator, you have to swipe your key in order to make the car go up." I felt so out of place, but I was trying not to look it.

"Your key will permit you to go to your floor, nine; the roof, which is where the infinity pool and barbeques are located; the lobby; and floor four, the workout and spa center. If you wish to access a different floor to visit someone, you will need to come to the concierge in order to receive permission."

I must have been giving him some sort of a blank stare

because he added, "We have high-profile residents here at Beach Tower—such as your mother, for example—and we find that our residents like to maintain their privacy."

"Of course. That makes sense." I tried to smile convincingly.

The elevator stopped. "Alright, here we are." The gold doors opened, and a cream-colored hallway appeared before us. A miniature version of the mirror-and-orchid display was arranged in the middle of the hall. "Now, just to the left, and we have Apartment 903. Welcome." George escorted me down the hall and pushed open a heavy, white, wooden door, revealing my new home.

The first thing I noticed was that everything was white. The second thing I noticed was that blocking my view to the ocean, which I knew was right in front of me, was Pam Michaels, Joey's mother and a longtime friend of my mom's. She stood, one hand on her hip and the other in the air, pointing. Today she wore skinny jeans, loafers, and a boxy bright red blazer. Her lipstick matched her jacket, in bold contrast to her carefully fake-baked skin. "Put that down there. No, a little to the left. Yes, yes, that's it. Good. Perfect." Pam was an interior designer. She held her arm out, directing movers who were holding up a big white couch and moving it inches to the left, then to the right until it reached its perfect position. When Pam was satisfied, she clapped her hands together and turned around to face me. "Becky! Great to see you. Now, what do you think of this amazing new furniture? Amazing, right?"

In front of me were boxes and brand-new tables, vases, and lamps. In just two weeks, my mother had furnished an entire apartment.

Pam walked me through a pile of furniture, asking if this desk would do, and how about those sheets? And what do we think of our new bed? Great, glad you like it. Now, moving on.

I saw Jack sitting on the floor of a bedroom—his bedroom, I guessed—listening to his iPod and looking at the wall. "Hey," I said, standing at the door to the room.

"This sucks," Jack said.

"Yeah." I nodded in agreement.

"Mom's in her room. It's at the end of the hall."

"Thanks." I dropped my backpack on the floor of the hallway and walked toward my mother's new bedroom. Mom was on her knees, digging through brown cardboard moving boxes, her hair tied up in a ponytail and the sleeves of her button-down shirt rolled up.

"Becky. Hi, sweetheart. Did your appointment with Sara Elder go okay?"

I shrugged.

"Have you seen your bedroom? It's gorgeous—has an ocean view. I think you'll like it."

I nodded. I had planned on talking to my mother, telling her about my day and my issues with Sara Elder, but suddenly, I found a nod was all I could manage. Anything more, and I was scared that I'd end up in tears.

I walked into my new bedroom, which was empty

except for an almond-colored desk and a full-sized bed. True to their word (although I couldn't figure out when or how), the valets had brought up my bags, and I dragged them into the empty walk-in closet. Sitting on the floor of my closet, I unfolded a shirt—only to realize that the closet had no shelves, drawers, or hangers. I put my head in my hands and began to cry.

Neverland

*T*wo days later, I was driving to school from Mom's new apartment when my cell phone rang. I was still trying to get the hang of the trip from Santa Monica to Hancock Park. My first day, I had arrived at school late enough to miss Advisory and most of first period, and I couldn't stand being late. I pressed down on the brake as I approached a red light and lifted my cell phone up to my ear. "Hello?"

"It's Mom. Did you call Rite Aid for a refill yesterday?"

I had left half an hour too early, and five minutes later I was just blocks from school—and so anxious that both of my legs were shaking.

Rite Aid was refusing to fill my Topamax prescription.

"It's against their store policy to aid a sixteen-year-old in the consumption of dangerous amounts of pharmaceuticals," my mom told me. Apparently I was being prescribed enough Topamax to overmedicate a horse. My mom was fuming and finally sputtered, "And it's against family policy to see a psychiatrist who would prescribe that amount."

The word *family* stuck out to me; I couldn't help thinking, *Does that word still apply to us?*

I turned onto my dad's street and haphazardly parked in front of the house. Dad might wonder what the hell I was doing there, but I needed to sit and think. And there was no room for doing any of that at school. Jack was at Dad's that morning despite the fact that we were supposed to be on our new schedule of one week with my mom and one week with my dad. It was his first day of school, so he'd wanted to be close to Stratfield.

I left my backpack in the car and walked silently into the house and up the stairs to my bedroom. "Hello? Becky?" Dad called out as I shut my door.

"Yeah," I answered, offering no further explanation for my unexpected arrival.

I sank into the corner of the room where the bookcase full of my old textbooks met the crate full of stuffed animals that I had insisted on keeping. I picked up a stuffed bear and clutched it in my arms. What about all my secrets? What about everything that I had told Sara Elder? Wasn't she supposed to want to help me, not hurt me?

I remembered how, when I was really little, I used to

take all my stuffed animals out of their shelves, boxes, and storage bins and put them on the floor of my room. I would hide myself among them. I was small. I was still just a little girl.

Now I was big, hiding in a corner of my bedroom, calculus and chemistry books jutting out from the bookcase that I was leaning against and poking me in the back. I held the soft bear close to my chest.

Jack walked into the room through the bathroom that he and I shared. "What's going on? Why are you here?" His hands were on his hips, and he looked around the room, trying to find me. "And why are you in the corner?"

Because my shrink is trying to hurt me.

Because I want to be five again.

"None of your business. Leave me alone."

"Why?"

Jack was waiting for something from me—a response, a shout, anything. But I stayed silent, and finally, he left. When I was alone once more, I poured all the stuffed animals out of the crate and onto the floor in front of me. I was bigger, and the animals were smaller, so it would be harder to hide. I opened my arms wide and pulled all the toys close together on top of me. Slouching down along the wall, I tried to bury myself with the past.

Blank Slate

*M*om and Dad were busy searching for a new psychiatrist for me, and I was busy trying to keep my school life together. I wasn't going to be seeing Sara Elder anymore. She had been my psychiatrist for five years, and suddenly, no more.

And I couldn't even figure out whether I was mad, sad, or anything. Sara Elder sent me an e-mail, maybe it was an apology or explanation—who knows. I deleted it.

My in-box was empty; I could be a new Becky, ready for change. A Becky who didn't need to pop pills both morning and night in order to be sane. A Becky who didn't necessarily need a therapist.

Neither of my parents believed my claim about not

needing a therapist. They supported me being whomever I wanted to be, but they just weren't sure that I could successfully be *me* without the aid of a psychiatrist. Throughout the next week, I couldn't help feeling as though I were holding everything together by a thread.

"Families are impossible," Taylor Tremaine said to me over lunch one day. It was just her and me—we had the same free period, which happened to be right before lunch that day. We had spent Advisory that morning telling our seventh graders what was edible and what to steer clear of in the cafeteria, so we decided to take our extra-long lunch as far from the school cafeteria as possible. That's how I found myself sitting at a hole-in-the-wall Mexican restaurant that Taylor had insisted was simply "the best," talking about our families.

"My parents just split up, too," Taylor offered. "It made me feel like nothing will ever be the same, you know?"

I did know. "Yeah, it's just . . ." My voice faltered. I squeezed a lemon wedge into my Diet Coke. I wanted to talk to Taylor, wanted to tell her that I knew what it was like, having your entire world shaken up and thrown on the ground. But for some reason, I couldn't. I didn't know what my problem was. It was as if keeping my emotions bottled up inside gave me a sort of control—a sense of control I desperately wanted to preserve.

Smart vs. Pretty

*L*ater that week, I presented to the Parents Association.

I came home from school—to my mom's apartment—the day of the presentation, and found Jack taping a miniature video camera to the outside of our front door. "What the hell?" I asked.

"Madonna moved in down the hall!" he explained, reaching for the electrical tape on the floor. "I'm hoping she does something interesting in the hallway, and then I can take the video footage and make a fortune."

Inside, Mom was sitting cross-legged, rooting through a big box of shoes on the living room floor. "Fuck." She threw a pair of Manolo Blahniks to the side, and they landed near my feet where several other pairs already lay. I dropped my backpack onto the carpet. "Have you seen my Ferragamo flats? I can't find them anywhere."

"Uh, no, I haven't. Sorry." I waded carefully into the kitchen and opened the refrigerator. "So, tonight's my PA presentation," I told the parmesan cheese.

"Tonight? I thought it was next week!" Mom tossed a ballet slipper back into the box and ran a hand through her hair. "What time? At school?"

"Yeah, at school. At seven." I shut the refrigerator door and turned out to face her. "You're coming, right?"

Mom stood up. "Of course I'm coming! It's a big night for you." She walked over to me. "You don't have to wear your uniform tonight, do you? Because I just found the cutest shirt in my closet!" My mother was always "finding" things in her closet and on her shelves. She brought so many things home from her show that it was hard to keep track of it all, she said. Her closet used to be bigger, though—in Hancock Park. Now, there were boxes of shoes everywhere, and if you opened a kitchen cabinet, you just might find purses instead of coffee cups.

I wore the shirt, and on the drive over to school, I sat in Mom's passenger seat and reviewed my speech in my head. I was a good speaker, but despite a number of awards and compliments after MUN conferences, I often worried that I wasn't as good at it as Amanda was. Amanda had sounded upset on the phone when we'd talked the other day. She was upset that we—I—had been asked to make a presentation and she wasn't there to be a part of it.

At the meeting, my parents sat on opposite ends of the same row, which was horribly awkward for me. I wanted to push my dad in about ten seats, to shout at him, "Look! This is how you made her leave. By always sitting so goddamned far apart," even though I knew that didn't really make sense at all.

The parents at Whitbread put on just as much of a show as the students do. There's that saying—the apple doesn't fall far from the tree—and I think it just might be true. In Whitbread's case, the tree is generally over-Botoxed, over-exuberant, and constantly dressing as though she were twenty years younger. Unless, of course, it is the case of the second wife. Those women actually are a full, inappropriate twenty years younger. The dads, well, they don't tend to come to PA meetings as much, but they are present at big school functions and have such big names that it's easy to forget celebrity isn't the norm.

The director of college counseling made an announcement about encouraging girls to add more activism and community service into their schedules. That was my cue.

I successfully held the attention of the parents in the room, and after I was done speaking, I ducked outside into the semicrisp September air. I headed to the Murphy Fountain courtyard and settled down in a light brown wicker chair, ready to leave, and waited for my mom to come outside.

"I can't believe I had to miss *Grey's Anatomy*. You have

to tell me about everything that happened," a woman squealed. I was tucked behind a big bush and couldn't see who was speaking. For a moment I thought that the voice belonged to one of my classmates, and that she was talking to me. I shot my head above the bush for just a moment. There was a woman carefully picking the sprinkles off a cookie, standing at the tableclothed snack table, her back to me. It was impossible to tell who she was—the patent leather heels and designer skinny jeans were entirely generic among Whitbread women—and she could've been anyone's mother, or stepmother or . . . older sister.

"This meeting is pretty boring," the mystery woman continued. "Oh! But there is one thing that your dad and I wanted to tell you." (Ah, a mother or stepmother, then.) "The college counselor spoke tonight about how extracurricular activities are so important. Are you in a club?" There was a pause, and I sat back down in the chair. This conversation probably wasn't worth snooping on. "Okay, well, your dad and I think that joining a club might be a really good idea, since you failed science last year and all, you know, because of all that time you had to take off after the boob job." I immediately perked up. *Failing? Boob job? Who?* "No, I know you did summer school," the woman continued. "Well, you had to. But anyway, I think you should join a club. Colleges are impressed with that sort of thing. And I know just which one you should join." I sat perfectly still, hoping that whoever it was didn't see me. "Oh, I agree, you shouldn't join a club full of nerds. No, of course not!" The woman paused for a response. "But there's a girl who spoke tonight."

I held my breath.

"She's president of Mock United Nations, I think that's what it's called, and she's very pretty. Doesn't look like a nerd at all. Plus, you get to go to conferences with boys—how's that for community service?"

I gasped. Even though this mystery woman's principles disgusted me, I felt my heart thumping with pride.

I, Becky Miller, was *pretty*?

Genius

$\mathcal{M}$y parents decided to send me to Miles Watson, who worked out of his home, which was deep in the Valley (an outpost of Los Angeles that I never drove to unless absolutely necessary). My brother had seen Dr. Watson. This was how he had been diagnosed with attention deficit disorder. My dad came to the appointment with me, even though I'd begged him not to. I think he was feeling guilty about not spending enough time with me. As if this were going to be quality time.

The house was large and white and covered with odd trinkets. On top of the coffee table, Christmas ornaments were scattered. Dr. Watson greeted us at the front door. He seemed to be in his late sixties and was very mild-mannered. His white hair was parted to the side.

He said that before he could treat me, he had to run a bunch of tests.

"So, today I will start by doing some general intelligence tests," Dr. Watson explained, speaking with careful enunciation. "We'll do the psychological tests, as well as the Wechsler IQ . . ."

I stopped him. "IQ? Why?"

"This is just the full battery of tests," he said mildly, smoothing the pant legs of his khakis.

"Fine," I agreed, resigned. "But can you promise me that you won't tell my parents my IQ score?" I looked to my dad. He nodded. "For personal reasons," I added.

"Well, if that's okay with you," he said to my dad, "then it's fine with me."

"Fine with me," Dad said.

I was scared to take this test. I was scared that I wouldn't score high enough.

My mom had never taken an IQ test, but she had been valedictorian of her Ivy League college class. My dad had taken an IQ test, and the result was so high that he refused to tell my brother and me the exact number, fearing that we might be concerned about not living up to his standard. I had always been more or less happy not knowing my IQ because, with me, my dad's fears were warranted. I worried that I wasn't as smart as my parents. And now I had been roped into taking an IQ test, and there seemed to be nothing I could do about it.

When Dr. Watson sat me down at a wooden dining table in his kitchen, I wanted to call bullshit. A psychologist who worked out of his kitchen? How good could he possibly be?

Dr. Watson sat down with me and explained that he was going to list some numbers, and would I please repeat them to him?

"One, seven, five, four, six, nine, eight."

I looked away, toward the patio door, and listened to him say the numbers. I could almost visualize them in front of me.

"One, seven, five, four, six, nine, eight," I repeated.

The strings of numbers got longer, and then Dr. Watson said that he was going to give me a mixture of letters and numbers. Could I please repeat them to him in alphabetical and numerical order—letters first, numbers second?

"C, seven, G, nine, three, T."

I collected the numbers and the letters in my mind, rearranged them, then spoke them.

"C, G, T, three, seven, nine."

It was only after correctly rearranging and repeating a particularly long sequence that I realized that the strange sensation I was feeling was my mind actually working.

Soon I'd moved on to a four-hundred-question psychological evaluation. Some of the questions applied to me—"Do you often find that you are so anxious that you cannot sleep?"—and others, not so much—"Do you see and hear things that do not actually exist?"

At the end, Dr. Watson told me that my verbal IQ was a little over 150.

"What does that mean?" I realized that all I knew about IQs was that 100 was average.

"Well, that means that you are in the top half of the ninety-ninth percentile." Was it my imagination, or was Dr. Watson smiling at me? I hadn't seen him smile before.

"Wow," I said, trying to register the information. How could . . . top half-percentile . . . really? The one personal attribute that I had always held the most stock in was my intelligence. I was never athletic, or skinny, or social, or beautiful. But I was always smart. I just hadn't had any idea how smart.

"It might be something you want to tell your parents. You should be proud, Becky. You are really an exceptional young woman."

A few minutes later, as I was coming out of the bathroom, I heard Dr. Watson in the living room talking with my dad.

"Your daughter is very bright," Dr. Watson said.

"She sure is," my dad replied.

"No," Dr. Watson went on. "I don't think you understand. Her IQ is 155."

I couldn't believe it! I burst into the living room. "You broke my confidence! Doctors aren't supposed to do that," I reminded him. "You said you weren't going to tell my parents." I stood with my hands on my hips, a few feet away from Dr. Watson's leather armchair.

Dr. Watson put his hand over his mouth. "I am so sorry, Becky. That was—that was really wrong of me. I just got so excited. . . ." I gave him a hard look. "I don't know what I can say; I really do apologize." His cheeks were pink; he was flustered.

My eyes burning, I concentrated on taking deep breaths as I followed my dad out the front door.

MUN

*A*t the first MUN meeting of the year, I was standing at the front of Mr. Elwright's classroom explaining parliamentary procedure to the twenty girls who'd shown up, when the door swung open and the Trinity walked in. Alissa led, casually carrying a Spago to-go bag in one hand and a large Louis Vuitton tote bag in the other. Kimberly followed with Courtney close behind, frantically skimming her *Norton Anthology of English Literature*. She wasn't an intellectual, but she was in my AP English class—and she was most likely behind on homework.

"Hey, sorry we're late. I had to wait for my driver to come and drop off our lunches." Alissa waved the Spago bag in the air and flashed a smile. Mr. E. shot me a look, as if to say, "Look who showed up."

"That's okay. I'm glad you could make it," I said, not totally sincerely. I resented these girls a little. Not only were they insipid and way too appearance-oriented, but they also had never been especially nice to me. I couldn't help wondering what they were doing at an MUN meeting.

Everyone listened attentively while I explained the rules of MUN conferences, but I heard a few excited murmurs when I told them about the first conference, up in Berkeley. It was a couple months away, but I was pretty excited about it, too. It would be my first big act without Amanda. I wanted to win an award. I wanted to prove that I was whole, and just as capable, without her.

When the lunch period ended, the Trinity descended upon me at the front of the classroom.

"This sounds like fun. You're such a good public speaker," Courtney said, probably referring to the video clip I had shown from a past conference. "Maybe you can help me out with my speechmaking skills. I'm not that great at it—not in front of big crowds, at least."

"Yeah, I can help you out," I said, trying not to let my confusion show. Part of me wanted to beam—Courtney Gross wanted *me* to do something with her? But the other part of me knew better, knew that there must be some underlying motive. And it probably wasn't that she was dying to be my friend.

I knew better than that. Besides, I didn't *really* want to be friends with the Trinity, did I?

"I can't wait to go to conferences with cute boys in suits," Kim added.

I grimaced. So there was an underlying motive after all.

Alissa pulled on Courtney's arm. "Guys, we have to go. The bell rang. See you in math, Becky!"

Despite my misgivings, driving home from school that day, I surprised myself by thinking that maybe, just maybe, this wouldn't be my worst year ever after all.

The Dating Game

I hadn't considered the possibility that my parents might start dating. The thought of my mom and my dad having sex with each other was hideous, but the thought of each of them having sex with other people—well, that was much worse.

One night I was in the kitchen, peeling an orange (I have to do it all in one piece, or else I can't eat the orange), when I heard my mom yell something from her bedroom. When I had finished peeling, I took the orange and went to see what was going on. I found her hunched over her computer monitor, staring at the screen.

"What's going on?" I asked, edging up against the desk.

"I just . . . got this message . . . from '2Fast2Furious.' I can't believe it."

She had signed up for JDate the week before, but she told me that she was just looking, just browsing other people's profiles, and that if she ever were going to go on a date, she would make sure to let me know beforehand.

"Why not, Mom? You're hot."

"It's . . . Harold!"

I looked at the screen. JDate's mail screen was up on the Web browser, and the following message was displayed in the center of the page.

From: 2Fast2Furious
Subject: Hey there!

Hey, smartblonde. I read your profile and user info, and you seem very interesting . . . even without a picture posted. Although you're a *little* bit outside my desired age range, I would really like to get to know you better. Please see a picture of me attached below. If you like what you see, don't hesitate to message back. . . . ;)

–2Fast2Furious

And below was a picture of a man in a baseball cap. A picture of my father. My Yankees-obsessed, BlackBerry-addicted *dad*.

So I did the only reasonable thing to do in such a situation.

I screamed. "What the *fuck*?! Outside his age range?!

What is his age range? I can't believe he's on JDate, too! And sharing his photo?"

Mom gave a disgusted sigh and pointed an impeccably painted nail at the screen. "It says here that he's more into the twenty- and thirty-year-old set. Natural blondes preferred."

"So, my dad is dating twelve-year-olds."

Courtney Gross's eyes widened in surprise.

"No, no, not literal twelve-year-olds. More like twenty-two-year-olds."

An MUN meeting had just ended and most of the girls had decided to stay in Mr. Elwright's room to eat lunch. I had dared myself to sit down with the Trinity.

"Ugh. I know what you mean," Courtney said as she dug a fork into the herb-roasted chicken breast in her Tupperware container.

Alissa was taking her time chewing a single baby carrot. Her feet were tapping rapidly on the floor. She swallowed the last bite slowly and said, "Omigod, your stepmom is hilarious!"

"Stepmom?" I asked. It was amazing how much I didn't know about someone I had gone to school with for almost five years.

"Yeah." Courtney sighed.

"She's, like, twenty-five, and all she does is shop," Alissa explained, clearly hating that the discussion wasn't focused on her. "Sometimes she'll drop by school in the middle of one of her very busy afternoons to get Court's opinion on a pair of shoes or something. I think she thinks that's stepmother-daughter bonding."

Courtney looked annoyed at Alissa, but then said to me, "So, I guess you have that to look forward to," and laughed uncomfortably.

"Yeah, it's pretty horrific," I agreed.

Kim gave me a wide-eyed look. "Wow. Are you like into studying vocabulary for fun or something?" Kim was notoriously stupid.

"Bitch! That's mean." Alissa poked Kim with her elbow. "What she means is that it's cool you use such big words in normal conversation. I was talking to this actress last night at dinner, and all she said was 'super cool'."

"Yeah. I bet you'll do really well on the SATs and stuff," Courtney chimed in.

I didn't mention how I had almost lost it when I missed one word on a first-grade spelling test. It was the only word I'd missed all year, and I thought it might ruin my record. Kim had gone to elementary school with me, but she'd clearly forgotten about this. I just nodded, said thank you, and speared another strawberry with my fork, trying not to think about what parental dating horrors might await me.

Meet the New Becky,
Same as the Old Becky

*H*ere's what my days and nights look like on Mom's weeks:

Wake up at 6:05 to shower, get dressed, and make the thirty-minute drive to school. Take Jack with me and drop him off at Stratfield, unless he had whined his way into staying at Dad's so he could sleep later. Go to school and try to fit in, which means not hiding in Mr. Elwright's class during free periods, but instead hanging out with Taylor or sitting with the Trinity and talking about (a) boys, (b) clothes, or (c) which clothes to wear when we might see boys. Or about the Trinity's exciting nights, when they go to expensive, extravagant parties, mingle with boring but attractive stars, dressed in sequined minidresses from Beverly Hills sample sales, and hook up with male models who were too strung out to remember their names. Even though my parents were big shots, my mom hated the celebrity social scene, and my dad never took me to whatever events he attended. Nights for me now involved some combination of traffic on the way to Santa Monica, homework, and maybe renting a movie with Taylor. . . .

Here's what my days and nights look like on Dad's weeks:

Get up at 6:35 to shower, get dressed, and make the short drive to school. Get home early, and then get depressed about being home alone in a big, empty house with nothing to do but read and watch television—or Google the Trinity and feel jealous about the exciting lives they were leading. Sometimes, one of the Trinity would instant message me and send me a picture of what she was wearing out that night. They didn't quite get that my life wasn't as illustrious as theirs, and I wasn't eager to correct their assumptions.

Here's how I feel no matter whose week it is:

Like I am missing something, constantly one step out of the loop.

Like I want to be somewhere else, living someone else's life.

Like I don't want to have to deal with Becky Miller and all her issues.

* * *

"You're becoming one of those popular sluts, aren't you?"
Amanda asked me one time after I had rehashed my day
with her over the phone. I told her about how I had gone
out to Mozza for lunch with the Trinity, and how Courtney and I had started sitting together in the Room during
free periods. First, I had told her about Taylor, that she
was nice and not quite as weird as we had supposed her to
be. To that, Amanda had replied, "No way. She's a freak,
Becky! Have you noticed that she sometimes goes without
a bra? Or maybe that was just a tenth-grade thing." I had
muttered "mm-hm" and quickly tried to change the subject. Now, I talked about my dare-I-call-it-friendship with
the Trinity instead.

"I am not!" I lay back in my bed, secretly pleased
that Amanda might be nervous that I was becoming one
of them—that I was *capable* of becoming one of them.
Amanda and I talked once weekly, at best. More often,
we just instant messaged. I was afraid that, with the physical distance between us, we might be growing apart. "I
wouldn't leave you for them," I added.

"No, don't worry, it's totally a good thing."

Did she really think that it was a good thing?

"Yeah, I mean, I've got a bunch of new friends here,
and I've been hooking up with this really cute guy for the
past few weeks. Oh, and I made the volleyball team!"

"Congrats!" I told her, trying not to resent the fact

that she knew boys—went to school with boys, even—and I didn't.

"Oh, and get this! Some of my new friends on the team invited me to go with them to this crazy Halloween party." I had completely forgotten that Halloween was coming up. "Speaking of," Amanda continued, "are you going to Pimps and Hos this year? You should. I bet your new friends could get you an invite."

Pimps and Hos was Whitbread's most notorious party. Every year, one upper schooler hosted, and because of all the money flying around at my school, each year's party was more elaborate and ridiculous than the past year's. Or so I heard. The idea was that guys dressed like pimps of some sort, and girls dressed like hos. Because Halloween was, after all, basically just an occasion for girls who were usually decently covered up to dress, and act, like sluts.

"Yeah, um, maybe I'll go. Who knows?" What I meant was, "Who knows if I'll even be invited?" I wasn't so sure that I was officially friends with the Trinity. Not yet, at least.

"Okay. You totally should, though. I'm dressing up as a Nava-ho for my Halloween party. It's going to be so cool. No parental supervision, a full bar. It's a real high school party!"

I took a deep gulp in. My idea of an exciting night was renting a movie and watching it at home with Taylor. That was fun in its own way, but it wasn't helping me grow socially or meet any boys. If I just sat around and waited, I might never get what I wanted. I figured maybe I had to make the effort.

A real high school party. Maybe that was just what I needed to push me in the right direction.

June Kauffman

I wonder if there's a rule that says all psychiatrist offices have to be either beige or full of ultramod glass. Maybe this "soothing" design scheme was created to provide a contrast to the vibrantly crazy people who frequent the offices. Maybe I'm one of them. But I don't find the design scheme particularly soothing.

June Kauffman came highly recommended by my mother's psychiatrist. I wasn't particularly nice to her the first time we met, but it's not like I was so hot on shrinks right then.

Before June Kauffman, and after Sara Elder, there had been Dr. Watson, who had pretty much betrayed me, as well as Dr. Rosenberg, who had asked me about which medications I was on. As a joke, I'd included Claritin in the mix, at which point he decided that Claritin was the root of all my problems and forbade me to take it. I didn't believe a word he said, but just to be safe I stopped taking it for a few days, and the only thing that happened was that I sneezed a lot more.

June Kauffman's office was just down the street from Sara Elder's, so I walked quickly into the building, with my head down. Her waiting room had several straight-backed wooden chairs that surrounded a beige plaid couch. The coffee table was oak-colored and worn down, topped with copies of *Architectural Digest*. Was this a theme, too—resoundingly unexciting choices in magazine subscriptions?

Dr. Kauffman looked like a younger version of Grandma Elsie, which terrified me a little. Her hair was single-process blonde, and she was about two inches wide. Her face was softer, though, and her lips weren't drawn in that hard line of Raspberry Passion lipstick. "Nice to meet you. I'm June, or Dr. Kauffman, whichever you'd prefer," she said as she led me down the short hallway to her equally beige office. Then she asked how I was. I didn't answer because it seemed like a ridiculous question. I sat down on the couch, right on top of the crack between the two sofa cushions. If I hid the cracks, maybe everything would just put itself back together again.

June asked me again how I was.

"Just great, really. My last shrink prescribed me enough Topamax to harm a horse, I tend to overcommit myself, my parents just separated, and yesterday, I put my house key in the car ignition by mistake. So I'd say I'm doing really well." I crossed my arms.

"Why do you think you feel the need to be so sarcastic? Could it be a way of protecting yourself?"

Was I that transparent? "I'm not being sarcastic," I said. "I'm just telling the truth."

"What medicines have you taken?"

"What medicines haven't I taken," I replied, rolling my eyes over to the river landscape on the opposing wall. "Really. I can't remember all of them."

"Tell me what you can remember. It's important that I know." She crossed her thin, stocking-clad legs and sat upright in the tall, dark blue armchair. That was the only piece of furniture in the room that wasn't beige.

I spoke to the floor. "Prozac, Zoloft, Effexor, Tenex, Clonidine, Topamax, Xanax, Valium, Wellbutrin, Ambien." That was most of them.

"Ambien? Who gave you sleeping pills?"

"Sara Elder, when I was in sixth grade."

"That's dangerous!" June Kauffman's glasses dropped down on her nose a little. She sounded outraged.

I shrugged and gripped my arms together tightly, wrapping them across my stomach. "I guess shrinks aren't that trustworthy."

"Becky," she said. "I'm not Sara Elder. And I'm sorry that you had such a bad experience, but I hope that you'll trust me when I say that I would never do anything to hurt you." I stared at the wall, making sure not to look June Kauffman in the eye. "The first thing I want to do, if it's okay with you, is take your dosage down on some of these meds. How does that sound? Can we work with that?"

It sounded pretty great.

The Ladies

I was online trying to find at least one Halloween costume that didn't involve showing massive amounts of skin, when Mom called me into the kitchen and announced she was looking for a new apartment.

"We just need more space!" she exclaimed, after opening a kitchen cabinet only to have a pile of high heels fall out of it and onto the counter. "Look at this!" She held up a red stiletto. "Not only is there nowhere to put my shoes, but I have absolutely no idea where the big serving bowls are, and the ladies are coming over in an hour!"

The "ladies" were the members of the Hollywood Women's Political Committee, and this would be the first meeting held at Beach Tower.

"Being at the beach is great," she told me, "but this is a little cramped."

An hour later, our living room was full of chattering women. And, to my surprise, Joey was there. When we had been little, Joey had often come to HWPC meetings with his mom, and while the women talked, we played in my room. But now that we were older and busier, he rarely showed up.

"Hey, Becky!" he said, catching sight of me sitting on one of the kitchen barstools. He gave me a wave, so I hopped off the stool and headed over to say hello.

"Becky, darling. I was just telling Joey how absolutely magnificent the new apartment is. Isn't it great, sweetheart?" Pam nodded toward Joey and then flashed me a bright red smile.

"Yeah," I said to Pam as she turned around to talk with my mom. Then to Joey I said, "Um, it's a surprise to see you!"

"Well, Mom just got a manicure, and her nails were still wet, so I offered to drive her." He smiled sheepishly.

Was it just me, or was that excuse really lame? Was it possible that Joey came just to see me? I felt something flutter within me.

"You look really good, Becky," Joey added. I remembered that Joey hadn't seen me since I changed my hair. Self-consciously, I tucked a strand of blonde hair behind my ear.

"Thanks," I said, genuinely meaning it.

"Doesn't she look fabulous?" Pam gushed, tuning back into the conversation.

Trying to escape the awkward moment, Joey changed the subject. "Where's your room?"

"Down the hall," I replied. Suddenly, I was a little nervous. I led Joey down the hallway and into my room, where Jack was on my computer. "Hey! What are you doing with that? You have your own, you know." I pushed Jack off of my desk chair.

"Yeah, but I'm downloading something on my computer right now. You weren't using yours, so . . ." He put his hands on his hips. "Hey, Joey. I have some pretty good movies if you want to watch." Jack winked at Joey. "You wouldn't be interested in them, Becky. Probably not your kind of entertainment, although you never know! After all, you had a pretty interesting web site up on your screen when I came in here." He laughed, and Joey fidgeted his legs.

I shot Jack a dirty look.

"Um, no thanks. I think I'll just hang out . . ." Joey began.

"Up to you." Jack shrugged. "But Becky, that definitely was quite a web site you were browsing!"

"It's none of your business! It's my computer; I can do whatever I want on it." *Please,* I thought, *please don't say it out loud. Please, not right now.* I was pretty sure that I didn't like Joey that way, but still. My life was already Embarrassment Central—I didn't need it to get any worse.

"What was on there?" Joey asked, shooting me a boyish grin.

Ugh. Bad question, bad question.

"Leg Avenue!" Jack shouted with glee. "Becky's looking at slutty Halloween costumes! What are you going to do, trick or treat at the Orthodox houses in Hancock Park dressed as a kinky French maid?"

"Um." I couldn't think of anything else to say. Plus, since when did my baby brother know what "kinky" meant?

"Okay, I'm out. I have business to attend to." Jack scooted out the door while I stood, staring at the dark computer screen, frozen.

I sank down to a sitting position on the floor, and Joey followed suit. "Are you going to Pimps and Hos?" he asked me.

"Maybe. I'm not sure yet," I said, pulling at the loose strings in the woven, rainbow-striped rug I'd bought to break up the monotony of the room. I didn't add that I didn't know if I'd even be on the guest list.

"I had no idea you were, you know, into that sort of thing." Most of the boys at Pimps and Hos, and any other Whitbread party, came from Stratfield, so Joey knew all about it. There was no "list" for boys for Pimps and Hos—Whitbread parties naturally had a high girl-to-boy ratio, so the girls throwing the party tended to be less exclusive when it came to which boys were invited. Joey ran a hand through his hair. "I was thinking of going," he added, "but I'm not that into the drinking scene."

I nodded. "It might be fun to do something different for a change." The truth was, I'd never been drunk—well, not in a party situation, at least. But I didn't need to expose myself as totally innocent.

"Yeah, maybe. So, you think you'll be on the list?"

"Hopefully. I don't know." I stood up, feeling a little awkward. "I'm going to go get a soda. Do you want anything?" I asked.

Joey stood up next to me. "I'll come with you."

We walked down the hallway silently, and after waving and saying hellos to the HWPC women, we slipped into the kitchen, which was just an extension of the living room. There were only two walls in the kitchen, and the view of the Pacific Ocean was uninterrupted. I passed Joey a Sprite and took a Diet Coke for myself. I popped the top off my soda, and Joey said, "You know, I think the biggest problem I have with P & H is that it's basically just an excuse for girls to dress up like sluts and guys to ogle them. It objectifies women." He shook his head.

I didn't disagree with him.

But was it bad that I sort of, kind of wanted to be one of those ogled girls? I could still maintain my self-respect while dressed like a slutty fairy-tale character, right?

"What was that?" Laura Turner, Kim's mom, called out to us, breaking away from the discussion of a married senator's affair with a call girl and craning her neck to see us. I elbowed Joey in the side, and he looked at me, confused. "Did you say P & H? I wish Kim would tell me what that stands for." Laura always wore pearls, and today was no exception. She turned back around to face the other ladies. "My daughter is throwing a Halloween party this year. It's called P & H, she says. She insists that I rent out the Key Club for the party. It's absolutely necessary, she tells me."

So it was Kim who was throwing this year's party. Getting an invitation should be doable, then. But why hadn't she mentioned it yet?

"What do you kids think?" Laura asked, turning to face us again. "Should I do it? Should I rent out the club for her?"

Joey elbowed me back.

"Well, I mean, I don't know. I hear it's a fun party," I said.

"Yes, Kim tells me it's some sort of school tradition."

"Yeah. I'd totally go, it's just, I don't know if I'm going to be on the list." The second the words were out of my mouth, I wished I could take them back. It made me sound so pathetic.

"The list? Is this one of those parties where only the supposedly cool kids get to go?" my mom asked. All other discussion in the living room had ceased. "Oh, I used to hate those kinds of parties. I never got invited."

Laura's head shot to my mom, back to Joey and me, and then to my mom again. "That's no good, is it? Am I aiding my daughter in all that popularity stuff? I shouldn't rent a club for that, should I?"

"I have an idea." My mother smiled brightly, as if a spark had just gone off inside her head. "Why don't you tell Kim that you'll only rent out the club if she invites everyone. The whole grade." Mom winked at me. "Plus Joey, of course."

Joey nudged me. "Guess you're invited now," he said.

Yeah, I guess I was.

The Younger Woman

"So, I think my dad's dating younger women."

June sat across from me, one leg crossed on top of the other, and asked if I had met any of my father's dates. I said no. "So maybe he's just exploring. If he were dating someone seriously, he'd have you meet her, would he not?"

"Maybe. Maybe not. Who knows? It's not like I've ever been in this situation before."

"That's true. But try to remember, he is your dad. And no matter how much you might feel the opposite, you do love him. You might not like him right now, but you love him."

I sat still, feeling numb and confused. June knew that I was interested in help, but she also knew that my parents were making me come to see her. I wanted to take it all back, everything that was happening, and go back a few years. I wanted a normal, shrink-free childhood.

As if I'd conjured her into being by discussing the subject with June, it wasn't long before Darcy came into our lives. I guess Dad realized that since he was stuck with us through the weekend, and we were stuck with him, if he were going to go out on a date, he'd either have to cough up the truth or come up with a pretty good excuse.

Jack and I were in the sunroom, together but not actually talking. I was reading T. S. Eliot for English class, and Jack probably should have been doing homework, too, but instead he was reading *PC Gamer* magazine, his legs propped up on the crayon-scribbled coffee table. His skinny legs poked out of his sagging shorts, and he had a do-rag on his head, covered with the hood of his sweatshirt. It wasn't even cold inside, but I guess that was what he thought completed his look. "Hey," I said, and he turned his head toward me slightly, his eyes peering out from under the hood. I was almost going to tell him about JDate, but his face looked so small. Jack was still little, I realized. He didn't need to be worrying or thinking about this crap.

The doorbell rang, and because we weren't expecting anyone, at least as far as I knew, I didn't rush to answer. Jack never answered the door unless forced to, so he continued to sit, silent and reading. "Hello!" I heard my dad call out as he opened the door. There was a pause, and I

wondered who it could be. "I want you to meet my kids."
My father's voice was growing louder as he drew closer. A
girl wearing skinny jeans and gold ballet flats entered the
room through the doorless archway; my father was right
next to her with his hand on the small of her back. She was
blonde and young, and her breasts were bigger than mine
would ever be. More important, this girl looked like she
could be my older sister—and not even by much. She was
definitely closer in age to me than to him.

Behind us, out the window, the sun was setting, melting
into burnt oranges and pale yellow-golds. I tried to focus
on the sunset instead of on the inappropriate couple that
stood before me.

I gave Jack a sharp look, wondering if he knew what
this was. He didn't meet my eyes, but instead continued
staring at the magazine page.

Dad introduced her as Darcy, saying that she was in the
entertainment business and had gone to NYU. They sat
on the couch opposite Jack and me, a respectable distance
apart from each other, and I wished I could install some
sort of magnetic field that would force them to remain
three feet apart permanently.

"So, Darcy, I bet you want to be an actress," I said.
Entertainment business, my ass. This girl just shouted
aspiring actress.

"Yeah, actually. I'm trying to break into the industry."

And she thought my dad could help her. She must not
have realized that dad's clients were mostly stars from

decades ago, and that he rarely attended industry events. She probably assumed that he would bring her to parties and premieres and introduce her to the hotshots of Hollywood.

"Dude, Dad, she looks like Maddie," Jack commented, giving Darcy the once-over from behind his magazine.

"Who's Maddie?" Darcy asked, looking nervously from Dad to Jack. I fought the urge to giggle.

"My girlfriend." Jack smiled. Maddie was a seventh grader at Whitbread. Even my little brother had a better social life than I did.

"Adorable," Darcy said, flashing her teeth in a smile. Darcy winked at me and folded her hands in her lap. "How old are you, Becky?"

"Sixteen," I answered.

"So you must be just starting the eleventh grade? That's cool." She grabbed onto my dad's elbow and flashed a look at her watch. She wanted to get out of here, probably, but even I knew that part of being a good girlfriend was pretending to like the kids. "I remember when I was in eleventh grade," Darcy nodded.

Yeah, of course you do, I thought. *That was only six years ago.*

There was nothing I could do to stop my dad from going out with her. And really, I guess I wanted him to be happy. What I didn't understand was why this Darcy business made *me* feel so empty inside.

Miss Popularity

*I*f there's one thing that moves quickly at Whitbread, it's gossip. Word about the nonexclusiveness of this year's Pimps and Hos party had spread fast. Kim had set up a Pimps and Hos group on Facebook, with a picture of the Key Club in the profile, and everyone was invited to join the group.

"Hey, are you going to Pimps and Hos?" I asked Taylor one morning during free period. This particular free period, I was lying on my stomach on the floor of the Room, checking the updates on the Facebook group.

"No way," Taylor said.

"Why not?" I asked. Taylor, if I remembered correctly, had worn a bikini onstage in a school production the year before. There was no way she had a problem with baring skin. Besides, her dad was a famous costume designer. He could probably make a pretty amazing costume for her. "Is it because of the drinking?" I asked.

"Nah. It's because it's stupid. It's just an excuse for girls who work too hard to play too hard, and totally show off while doing it. You and I both know that the morning after, there'll be tons of new pictures posted online of those girls in their underwear, prancing around with bottles of Jack Daniel's."

The truth was, I didn't like that Pimps and Hos was an excuse for girls to make sluts out of themselves and then giggle self-deprecatingly while guys treated them like the sluts they were pretending to be.

So why did I want to have a photo of *me* with Jack Daniel's online? Knowing all that I did, why did I still kind of want to be one of them?

"Totally," I said, agreeing with Taylor and quickly exiting the Facebook page. "It's pathetic." Taylor gave me a confused look. "And immature," I added. Taylor nodded. I wanted to make sure I had her approval as a level-headed, mature friend.

It seems I always want people to approve of me.

Later that day, Kim approached me in the hall. "Cute shoes."

I was wearing red, patent leather ballet flats, as a result of my mother's fashion advice. I made a mental note to thank her.

"Thanks," I said, smiling. Was I smiling too widely? Damn it. Why did I even care about whether Kim thought I was smiling appropriately? I looked up at her. She was really tall, and I always felt sort of stout around her.

"Are you coming to P & H? 'Cause you totally should."

I couldn't stop myself from nodding.

"Just RSVP on Facebook." The bell rang. "I should go. I have chem, and I missed yesterday for a sample sale. So, I'll see you at the party?"

"Yeah," I responded, standing still, trying to get my bearings.

Kim turned to leave, and then, as she began to head down the hallway, she turned around and added, "Cool. There's no list this year, but, if there were, you totally would have been on it."

I couldn't help feeling as though my social status might be changing. Being friends with Taylor was fine—but friends with the Trinity? Now that would be *amazing*. After all, this was high school. I had plenty of time to find friends who were my intellectual equals. Besides, partying at P & H seemed a hell of a lot more exciting than watching a movie with Taylor.

A few days later, Alissa invited me to go out to lunch with her, Kim, and Courtney. We sat at Matsuhisa, an expensive Beverly Hills sushi restaurant, nibbling on sashimi and rating the Stratfield boys who would be at the Halloween party. Seeing as I knew almost no boys, except for Joey, I had very little to contribute, aside from my excitement at the prospect of meeting some.

"The guys on the basketball team are pretty hot," Courtney said.

"Yeah, but not as hot as the soccer team!" Alissa chimed in as she took a tiny bite out of the single piece of sushi on her plate.

"Yeah, the soccer players are pretty cute," I added. I just hoped nobody would ask me if I actually knew any soccer players. I stared at the food in front of us on the table. We had ordered a lot, but most of the food sat uneaten in front of us. I was starving, but I didn't want to seem like a horse on my first real social outing with the group.

"Who do you know on the soccer team?" Alissa asked.

Shit.

I was about to speak, but Alissa quickly interrupted me. "Hey, I just remembered who *I* know on the soccer team! Aaron Winters. You guys probably don't know him because he's been out of the country for a couple years. I think he was in Switzerland. His mom was living there—said she needed a break from the 'Hollywood life.' But he's back, apparently, because his mom e-mailed my dad and said that I should introduce him to some new friends. He's at Stratfield, but he knows, like, no Whitbread girls." She stopped to take a breath. "I invited him to P & H, of course. But the thing is, I haven't seen him since, like, eighth grade, at one of my parents' parties." Alissa looked around the table to make sure that we were all paying attention. We were. "Anyway, I remember him being pretty cute. He played soccer back then, and I bet he's on the team this year. Who knows, maybe someone can get some action with him!"

A new boy? A new boy who wouldn't know or have heard all about my lackluster reputation as the Smart Girl? Yes!

Courtney looked down into her salad. Kim laughed. "Score! New blood. Sounds great."

"Yeah, because he won't already know your reputation," Alissa said.

I started to blush until I realized she was talking to Kim, not me.

"What reputation?" I asked, even though I knew. Amanda and I had referred to them as the Horny Trinity, after all. But was Kim somehow worse than the others? Kim elbowed Alissa and gave her a look of warning.

"Kim tends to get slutty when she drinks." Alissa smirked, then turned the smirk into a smile. She laughed, so I did, too, hoping that this was a joke and that it was the right thing to do.

I went to the bathroom before we left the restaurant. In the stall next to me, Alissa was doing something that sounded a lot like throwing up. As we washed our hands side by side, I knew better than to say anything. "You're looking good," she told me. The fact that such a little compliment made me so excited embarrassed me.

After Matsuhisa, I ate lunch with the Trinity on a fairly regular basis. I started seeing less of Taylor outside of Advisory. Every time she asked what I was up to, I would make up some school-related thing, usually having to do with MUN.

Within a week, Taylor joined MUN. She said she didn't know how much time she could spend researching, because of drama, but that since I talked about MUN all the time, she wanted to see what it was like.

I tried to include her, tried to make her feel welcome, but when, at the end of her first meeting, I sat down with Alissa, Courtney, and Kim to eat lunch, Taylor didn't join me.

"Why don't you come sit with us?" I asked, weakly. She didn't. The truth was, I could tell that the Trinity didn't especially like Taylor. And I didn't want them to not like me just because I was friends with her.

Later, Taylor was packing up her backpack, getting ready to leave. She looked like she had something to say, so I walked over to her.

"I like you, Becky, but them . . . They're fake, you know? They're nice to anyone who's nonthreatening and willing to go along with whatever they want to do. But if you don't act like a robot, then you're screwed."

I widened my eyes. Was Taylor calling me a robot?

"I'm not saying *you* are a robot," she corrected. "Just . . . if I were you, I wouldn't get too close."

I shrugged. Taylor was wrong. She just didn't want me to become better friends with them than I was with her. She was jealous—that was it.

Trick or Treat

I'd put off getting a costume for so long that by the time Halloween had arrived, I had nothing to wear. I had always been . . . creative with my costumes, as anyone who'd gone to elementary school with me could attest, but this year I just wanted to look like a normal teen girl. Which is probably why I'd procrastinated: Normal teen girls dressed like sluts for Halloween, and part of me really didn't want to give in to that.

"Alissa wants me to be a mouse because she's going as a cat, but I'm not sure," Courtney told me as we lay on the field at break, sipping nonfat lattes and alternating between gossiping and quizzing each other on ancient philosophers. It had taken Courtney twenty minutes to finally understand the difference between Plato and Socrates. Maybe sticking to gossip was the easier way to go.

"Yeah, that's a little weird," I said. "Cat and mouse? It's like some sort of power play. As if she has dominance over you . . . or she's chasing you, or something like that."

"I guess. Whatever—I can always just tell my stepmother to go out and buy something. That way, I'll be sure to look like the whore I'm not!"

There was no safe way to ask how much of a whore she wasn't, which is what I really wanted to know, so I just said, "Yeah, me either. And I don't know how I'm going to dress like one either."

"Who's not what?" Kim asked, settling down next to us on the Burberry blanket that covered the grass.

"Becky's not sure about dressing slutty for Halloween," Courtney said.

Kim let out a long laugh, cocking her head back in the air, her hair falling behind her. "I can believe that! You know . . ." she said to Courtney.

Please don't, I thought. *Please don't.*

". . . she dressed up as Hillary Clinton in the first grade!"

Thank you, Kim.

"Oh, and who were you in the sixth grade, again?" she asked me.

I tried to put on a good-hearted, self-deprecating smile. "Ralph Nader," I said. I had worn a suit with a tie that read

SPOILER. I stood up before things could get any worse. "Listen, guys, I have to go, but see you at lunch!"

As I walked off toward the history hallway, I heard the end of the conversation in the background.

"Who's Ralph Nader?" Courtney asked.

"Fuck if I know."

After school, I headed to Yes!, a novelty store and, come October, costume store. It was just down the block from what I'd started thinking of as Therapists' Row. I'd parked along the side street that was in between June Kauffman's and Sara Elder's buildings, and I quickened my pace as I passed both.

The store was packed with last-minute shoppers roaming the aisles of tacky costumes wrapped in plastic bags.

I waded through an aisle that was labeled WOMEN but looked more like it should say SLUTS. To my left, a girl slipped on a ladybug tube dress. "Can I help you?" a petite salesperson in a revealing Snow White costume asked me.

"I'm not exactly sure what I'm looking for," I said, suddenly wishing that I weren't wearing my school uniform.

The conversation I'd had with June the day before played in my head.

"Well, what do you want to dress up as?" she'd asked, when I told her I was stressing about what to wear to P & H. "What would you be *comfortable* dressing up as?"

I'd stared at the tapestry on the wall opposite me. "I don't know."

"Think about that. Think about Becky and what Becky wants. I want you to be able to smile in those Halloween photos."

The saleswoman—MARINA, her name tag said—chewed her gum noisily and gave me a once-over, then turned to the wall of costumes, picked one out, and handed it to me. I repeated June's question in my mind, and still came up with no answer. The cover of the costume bag pictured a very busty fake blonde wearing a baseball shirt, hat, and kneesocks. The shirt was red and white and cut in a deep V-neck. Down the front, it read PLAYER. I held the plastic handle tentatively. "Just try it on. It's really cute," Marina assured me.

I put my purse on the floor between my feet and removed the shirt from the plastic bag. At least I was short enough that the shirt might work passably as a dress. With the "costume" over my T-shirt, I searched the aisle for a mirror. If the costume was slimming, I might be able to deal with it saying PLAYER on the front. I would wear sneakers, not heels like the model in the picture. I made my way through girls in slutty Dorothy, Minnie Mouse, and 1950s girl costumes in order to reach the mirror.

"I like that one, Mom," a preteen girl proclaimed, pointing to me. She put her hands on her skinny hips and smiled up at her mother. "Especially the number on the back!"

"Honey, I'm not sure that's appropriate," the mother added.

I jerked my head around in terror to face the girl. "What number is it?"

"Sixty-nine."

Oh no. No. I was not going to walk around as an advertisement for oral sex. Not even if the shirt was slimming. I zigzagged my way back toward Marina and my uniform skirt, hopelessly trying to take the shirt off at the same time.

From behind me, I heard a familiar voice. "Yes, excuse me? Do you have this Little Red costume in a smaller size?" But then, amid the masses of teenagers and polyester, a bony hand emerged in front of me, waving frantically from the sleeve of an orange sweater set. It was rather distracting.

"Oh, now this is cute!" The woman in the orange sweater set held up a bumblebee costume and took a step toward the mirror, holding the outfit in front of her. "Honey, I think you'd like this."

Suddenly, the reflection of a middle-aged woman with curly blonde hair appeared in the mirror, next to the orange sweater set. "Yes, my niece says that she is looking for the Little Red costume in a size small."

It was none other than Sara Elder, contemplating the purchase of a Leg Avenue costume.

I ducked to the ground against the side of the aisle, where pieces of costumes had fallen and I stood a dangerously likely chance of being trampled upon. Grabbing onto the baseball shirt, I tried to tug it off, but from my fetal position on the ground, this was difficult to do.

The familiar mass of curly blonde hair attached to a babbling cell phone appeared precariously close to me. "Yes, dear, I'm looking for your size," Sara Elder spoke into the Nokia.

My former psychiatrist was shopping for a Little Red Riding Ho costume?

Still kneeling on the ground, I stretched my arm upward and grabbed for a costume bag. Lil' Ho Peep? This would work. The skirt was pictured as longer than crotch-length. Not exactly "what Becky wants," but I could make this work.

On the way home, I called Joey to ask him for a ride to the party. The only rule my parents had ever given me was that I wasn't allowed to drive past eleven at night.

"Sure," Joey said. "I might not stay very long, though."

I thanked him and flipped the phone shut.

When I arrived home, Dad, Jack, and Darcy were sitting around the coffee table in the living room on the newly recovered couches while the television hummed from the dark wood armoire. A bottle of white wine had been uncorked, and Jack's feet were up on the table as he sipped a Coke. The only signs of Halloween came from the lopsided pumpkin sitting right outside the front door and Jack's multicolored Afro, which stood up high in the air. Dad was still in a suit, and Darcy, well, her minidress was nothing out of the ordinary.

"Oh, good, Becky's here. Hey, Becky, why don't you spend some time with Darcy while I help Jack figure out his costume for tonight." My dad flashed me a grin and stood up, smoothing out his pant legs.

"What are you doing tonight, Becky? I'm so disappointed that I won't get to spend the night trick-or-treating with you!" Darcy's smile was too sugary to be sincere. She winked, grabbing onto Dad's elbow and standing up next to him. If she had turned around, she might have seen Jack casually raising his middle finger to her.

"I'm going to a party."

Jack stood up, and I realized exactly what my dad had meant about needing to rework his costume. It was impossible to tell what Jack was attempting to dress up as—rapper with an Afro, perhaps. He was wearing his shorts so low that his boxers were almost entirely visible. The problem was, he hardly looked tough, since his boxers were covered in lots of little starfish. Jack wore a Laker's hat on top of the Afro and wore a white T-shirt with a big "J-Zizzy" in black marker on the front. I managed to keep from laughing until he and my dad had made it up the stairs.

Then, it was just Darcy and me. Darcy looked down at her fingernails, alternating between examining her cuticles and checking her watch. "How long are they going to be?" she finally asked me, with dread hanging from her voice. Then, a minute later, she added, "So, what do you want to do? Um . . . we could . . . I don't know . . .

something." Maybe she thought this was some obligation she had to fulfill in order to win my dad's heart—and a starring part.

"Hey, so you finished school pretty recently, right?" I knew the answer, but I hoped the question might drive home my point. I walked into the front hallway and grabbed my backpack by the straps. I never did homework on Friday nights, but there was no way she would know that. "I have so much homework," I said, pretending to sound exasperated. "You know. So, I should probably get started on that." As casually as I could, I removed my calculus book and binder from my bag. "Lots of math to do."

"Oh. Okay."

I began circling my homework problems in the textbook. Darcy sat silently for a few minutes while I wrote out formulas. Finally, she said, "Do you want any help with that?" Her voice was entirely lackluster.

"Sure! Here, see if you can figure out problem twelve." I smiled brightly, passed the book over, and handed Darcy a sheet of paper and a pencil. Twelve was a relatively easy problem, no discontinuities in the function, and it was clearly differentiable. It was probably mean of me, but I resented Darcy. My dad went out with her all the time, but *I* got barely one night of his time a week.

"Right," she said slowly. She wasn't actually expecting me to take her up on the offer. "Okay, I guess. Where's the problem?" She tried to smile.

Darcy chewed on the eraser end of the pencil I had given her, and I continued my work, hunched over the coffee table. "Hey," she finally said, calling me up from my working position. She slammed the pencil down on the table and sat up straight. "What is this, calculus or something?" she asked.

I leaned across Darcy to where the textbook sat open on the table. I snapped the book shut. It was dark blue with big white writing. It read CALCULUS.

"Yeah," I said. "It *is* calculus."

"You know, I think I'm going to go check on your dad. It's probably time to get into our costumes!" She stood up nervously and had to pull down her skirt because it was riding up. Way up. "Okay, then," Darcy said, teetering away on her dark red stilettos.

I laid out the costume on top of my multicolored quilt. Lil' Ho Peep wore white and pink, but mostly white. The top was a sleeveless mock corset and was meant to come down to a little below waist level. On me, thanks to my lack of height, I hoped it would be longer. My stomach wasn't as unattractive as I used to think it was, but still. I was barely comfortable wearing a bikini. Lil' Ho Peep also wore a short skirt (white with an inch or so of pink trim along the bottom). The skirt had two layers, in order to suggest the existence of a petticoat, but the fabric was too thin to billow out successfully. The plastic costume bag also included a pink-and-white bonnet to be tied around the neck, as well as a long, hooked plastic cane.

I started by putting on bike shorts, just in case the skirt was too short, and a bra. This, I guessed, might be all that some girls were planning on wearing to the party. The top fit just fine, and I was thankful to have the corset to hold me in. Standing in front of the full-length mirror attached to my bedroom door, I pulled the cotton skirt up my legs, above my shorts. I raised the waist of the skirt to what I would normally view as uncomfortably high. The skirt met the hem of the corset right below my belly button, and it didn't leave any of my midriff showing. I walked to the mirror and turned to the side to examine my appearance. The skirt was really short. I was probably supposed to be wearing it at my hips, and that would have been fine except for the fact that the top ended at my belly button. Examining the skirt from behind, I decided that wearing it at the waist would have to do. Either way, I wasn't really at risk of looking too conservative in this outfit.

After pulling my hair out of its ponytail and brushing it out, I tied on the bonnet. With finishing touches of sparkly pink lip gloss and the peep-toe pumps I'd bought on my recent shopping trip with Mom, I was able to smile confidently in the mirror as I opened the door to head downstairs.

I actually looked pretty.

I approached the head of the stairs with a bounce in my step, ready, excited, and imagining how this Aaron guy might feel if he saw me. He, and every other boy there, knew nothing about me except what I would tell them. It was a magical thought.

The clicking of heels on the tile below snapped me out of my dream world.

"Oh my goodness. Great minds really do think alike!" From her perch on my dad's arm, Darcy forced a chuckle.

My first thought, as I stood with my heels glued to the carpet at the top of the stairs, was, *Oh, so* that's *how this costume is supposed to look.* My second thought was, *What the hell?*

At the bottom of the stairs, next to my dad in a magician's cape and my brother in, well, some sort of eccentric rapper outfit, was Darcy. Dressed as Lil' Ho Peep. Except, while I still sort of looked like a kid playing dress-up, Darcy looked like the real thing. Boobs, ass, belly button, and all.

I crossed my arms over the inch of my stomach that I realized had become exposed while I was walking. I tugged at the bottom of my top, blushing in the presence of Darcy's skin exposure.

So then my third thought was, *I have to get the hell out of here. Right now.*

P & H

*J*oey picked me up in his mother's old dark green minivan. I folded up my cane and climbed into the passenger seat, eager to get away. Joey wasn't wearing a costume, exactly. He wore dark-wash jeans with a white button-down shirt that was mostly unbuttoned, and for the first time, I realized that Joey was not just little Joey who played with trucks and didn't get mad easily. Joey was . . . well, he was actually kind of cute.

As we approached the Key Club, I saw the bright blue projection of a large, old-fashioned key and the marquee just below it, which usually boasted the names of bands playing gigs. Tonight, there were only three black characters, stark and just mysterious enough against the illuminated white background.

P & H.

An overweight bouncer sat on a folding chair in front of the door.

"Okay, this is it," I said, pulling on a black sweater as Joey parked in front of the valet stand. I suddenly felt very bare. I jerked my oversized pink cane sideways through the car door and tucked my cell phone into the side of my skirt. Then I got out of the minivan and walked with Joey toward the club. A couple of paparazzi, toting large cameras, stood a few yards away from the entrance.

"Hey! Who are you?" one of them called as Joey and I walked to the club. I smiled, but didn't answer, and followed Joey through the front entrance.

I pushed the heavy black door open and walked into the madness. Standing at the end of the entrance hallway were Alissa and Courtney. Both wore matching black lace bras and boy shorts and, underneath, different colors of fishnet tights. Alissa's were pink, Courtney's were blue. Both girls wore their hair in low pigtails, but while Alissa's blonde locks were straightened, Courtney's red hair frizzed out from beneath the rubber bands. Alissa wore a headband that had pointy white ears with pink centers on the top. Courtney's headband was similar, but instead of white, her ears were gray. Both wore knee-high black leather boots.

"Becky! Guess what I am." Courtney teetered over to me and wrapped her arms around me in a hug.

"A mouse?" I asked. She looked nothing like a mouse, and Alissa looked nothing like a cat, but when dressing like a slut, lingerie and a headband count as a costume.

"Yeah." Courtney nodded.

"See, I told you it was obvious!" Alissa said. "Come on, let's go mingle." Alissa grabbed one of my arms, and Courtney followed suit, grabbing onto the other. I looked around for Joey, but it was dark and I didn't see him. We walked, as a pack, across the main room of the Key Club. On the left side was a bar, which was officially shut down for the night because management knew that the club would be filled with underage kids. Even so, the countertop of the bar was covered with stacks of red plastic cups and bottles of various kinds of alcohol. Farther in, there was a stage, and Kim sat on the edge of it, holding court with a few girls and a group of guys, none of whom I could identify. She was wearing some sort of a baseball jersey. I couldn't tell how long it was but, from where she sat, most of her long, tan legs were exposed. Kim caught sight of me and the playboy cat and mouse, and jumped off of her perch. Her heels hit the black cement with a click. Alissa and Courtney began to move forward, toward the mass of teenagers. I followed but made sure to stay a step behind. My skirt was too short. My corset was riding up. What the hell was I doing here?

"This is, like, totally perfect. I'm so glad Mom agreed," Kim said as she approached us. She gave both Alissa and Courtney a kiss on each cheek, and then she approached me.

But here's the thing. I hug and kiss my parents all the time, and I really want to meet a boy, who could become my boyfriend, who I would love to kiss. But I'm basically awkward with physical displays of affection. Like the two-cheek kiss. It makes me feel entirely uncomfortable.

Kim reached in to give me a hug, and I responded by putting my arms gently around her back. The baseball jersey was silk, I noticed. "It's all thanks to you, Becky. You and your mom! Otherwise this would be in some crummy, so-last-season warehouse."

"This is pretty crazy!" I said, taking in the Nava-ho to my left (which made me wonder how Amanda's night was going), the shirtless boy holding a bottle of Absolut, and the smoky-sweet smell of pot.

"No, Becky, this isn't crazy," Alissa said, grabbing a hold of my hand again and directing me to the bar. "*This* is high school."

It certainly wasn't the high school *I* knew. I shrugged my shoulders out of my sweater and rearranged the cane in front of me.

"Hey, look, it's Lil' Ho Peep!" some guy called out. I turned around to find a guy wearing only striped boxers giving me a thumbs-up sign. My stomach clenched and I quickly turned back to the Trinity.

"Anyway," Kim said, tripping over one of her heels as she tried to take a step toward me, "we are totally going to drag you out from that encyclopedia you've been hiding under!" Her words were high-pitched and slightly slurred.

She grabbed onto my elbow, inadvertently pushing Alissa backward. Alissa stopped herself from falling by grabbing onto a railing. "And the first step is right this way!" We were a few feet from the makeshift bar.

Alissa didn't take well to being pushed out of the way. She brushed her fishnets off and stomped ahead. "Drunken slut," I heard her mutter. She went to stand behind the unattended bar. I stood with Kim and Courtney on the opposite side. "What's your pleasure?" Alissa asked, folding her arms over her chest.

"I'll take a vodka cranberry." Kim leaned forward and rested her head on her hand, which caused her ass to stick out. Way out.

"You're drunk enough," Courtney said. She turned to the side and tried to discreetly pull down her boy shorts. Half of her ass was exposed, only covered by her fishnets, and I could tell that this made her uncomfortable.

"Well, you're *not* drunk enough!" Kim replied.

"Okay, Courtney, what will it be?"

"Beer." She grabbed a can of light beer from a carton.

"That won't get you drunk, you know," Alissa said.

"I know," Courtney said.

"It'll just make you fat." Courtney's face sunk visibly. "Kidding!" Alissa continued. "You'll never be fat. You're a hottie."

"And what about Becky? She's totally sober."

"We can fix that. What do you want?"

I asked for a vodka tonic. The drink was presented to

me in a red plastic cup, and I took a bigger gulp than I should have, because I quickly began to feel the alcohol stinging my throat. I wasn't supposed to drink alcohol, not with the meds I was on, but the warmth spreading in my stomach just felt so good.

I remembered this feeling and relished it.

I had been completely drunk only once before. I was twelve and in the seventh grade. Too smart and too observant, I was nearly friendless. I sat at the dinner table, indignant that my parents seemed to have no concept of limits. They would randomly present me with things I didn't want (like clothes, electronic gadgets, dinners out at expensive restaurants) in order to show their love for me, in order to provide me with the things they hadn't had—and had pined for—as children. But when it came to things I really wanted from them—for them to show up at my school events without my having to remind them constantly, for them to notice that I was in pain, buried under depression—they fell completely short.

So, right in front of them during one of their competition-discussions about who was the most overworked, the most stressed, the most accomplished, I poured myself a glass of Grey Goose vodka and orange juice. With nine-year-old Jack preoccupied with his video games and with my parents preoccupied with their pressures, I felt invisible. I was sick of being perfect and good, capable and competent. I wanted them to notice. "I'm having some vodka," I told my parents, who didn't hear me—at least, they didn't stop me. So I went and poured another. And then another. And then I was drunk, delirious, and empowered.

I hadn't ever been that drunk since, because I knew that drinking alone was a sign of alcoholism. I was already a depressive obsessive-compulsive—I didn't want to risk adding another label to my list.

But now that vodka was presented to me in a social context, I jumped at it. It would, I reminded myself, make me stupider, which would in turn make me less self-conscious and more capable of getting along with my classmates. Taking a deep gulp of the fiery liquid, I smiled.

I knew that I shouldn't drink. It would fuck with my neurotransmitters. I would pee out all the meds, and in a few days I would feel like shit. But right at that moment, it seemed worth it. I wasn't sure that I would make it through the night any other way.

After a bit, I excused myself from the Trinity and took a lap around the club, looking for Joey. I found him standing with a boy dressed as a fireman. "Hey!" I said. "I had no idea where you went."

Joey introduced me to his friend, whose name was Chase, and then said that he thought he was going to head home before everyone's clothes came off completely.

"You'll be okay?" he asked. "You have a ride home?"

"Yeah," I told him. "Don't worry about me!"

"Have fun, and stay safe," he said.

Kim was walking toward us. "Joey. Hey," she said. Joey and Kim were acquaintances, because of their mothers, but they weren't friends. "Becky, come with me," Kim said, grabbing my elbow. It occurred to me that Kim might think she was saving me from some sort of social no-no.

A group of boys, all in different states of undress, entered the room. All I can remember is that every one of them had muscles—really nice muscles.

"The soccer team," Alissa exclaimed, her voice hushed.

"So, that guy you were talking about, Aaron Winters, is he here?" I asked. I leaned my cane against the bar and tried to appear calm.

"Shh!" I hadn't realized that I was talking so loudly. "He's right"—Alissa cocked her head up, toward a boy whose shaggy blond hair immediately stood out—"there."

The boy walked over to us and gave a hug to Alissa. "It's been a while," he said.

He was wearing drawstring khaki pants and essentially nothing else. There was a plastic silver sword attached by a holster to the right side of his pants. He had a six-pack, and I immediately decided that I was in lust.

After that everything went fuzzy.

I have a few distinct memories from the rest of the night, but that's it.

The first was after I had finished my third drink, and Courtney asked where I was spending the night. "My house," I told her. "I just have to call my dad when I want him to pick me up." I was too drunk to lie.

"You're not having your dad pick you up!" she exclaimed. I took another sip of my drink. "You'll stay at my house, with Alissa, Kim, and me. Okay?" I must have nodded yes.

The next conversation I remember was also with Courtney. We sat on round velvet ottomans, and I stared at Aaron, daring him to look my way. "That guy," I told Courtney, referring to a tall Tarzan on a couch across from us, "is giving you the *look*. He's cute. I bet you could totally hook up with him," I said.

She fiddled with the waistband of her fishnets and was quiet for a moment. "See, here's the thing. I might as well tell you now because they make fun of me for it all the time. But just nice fun. And, you're drunk, so who knows if you'll even remember. The thing is, I've never actually been kissed."

I almost coughed up the vodka-doused olive I had just swallowed. "Never been kissed?" I asked. How could cool and confident Courtney have never been kissed?

She nodded.

I took a deep breath and put down my drink. "Neither have I."

That's how I know I was drunk. If I were sober, I never would have divulged this sort of information.

"You know who's so hot? Aaron. Like, fuck-me-now hot," I said, leaning back on the ottoman and just barely remembering to make sure my skirt covered all the necessary areas.

"You should go talk to him. Say hello and stuff."

And because I was drunk, that's exactly what I did.

Aaron was leaning against a railing, his elbows drawn back behind him for support. His chin was cocked up, and when I approached, he was standing alone.

"Hi, I'm Becky." I walked over and offered him my overly perfumed right hand.

"Aaron," he replied.

"Nice to meet you. So, um, where do you go to school?" I knew the answer, of course, but nobody had warned me about how awkward I might feel trying to conduct a semiserious conversation while wearing this monstrosity of a costume.

"Stratfield. You're a Whitbread girl, right?" He smiled.

"Yeah, I go to Whitbread. So, what do you like to do? Like, what's one of your hobbies?" I pulled down at my skirt and inwardly scolded myself. That sounded a hell of a lot more like a college essay question than flirting.

A few minutes later, I was with Aaron at the bar, my hand interlaced with his, doing shots of Grey Goose.

The next scene I remember was Kim, Courtney, Alissa, Aaron, and me, all sitting around a low, glossed-wood coffee table. Alissa was kneeling over the table, mixing martinis for us.

As if we weren't drunk enough already.

"Hey." Aaron, sitting across from me, suddenly tapped my left foot with his. "Check this out." He held up a phone that was smaller and thinner than any phone I had seen before. "It hasn't come out yet. My dad got a demo version and gave it to me. Isn't it cool?"

Alissa laughed. "You better not be planning on getting any text messages from Becky; she's the slowest phone-typist in the world."

"I am not. You're just jealous of my spelling skills," I taunted back.

"Who spells things correctly when you're on a phone?" Courtney asked.

"Becky."

"Well, I'll just have to find out for myself, then, won't I? What's your phone number, Becky?" Aaron flipped open his phone and looked at me, his blue eyes looking intently into mine.

I was shivering with excitement, and the ceiling had begun to spin above me. It was all I could do to remember my own phone number. I think I gave him the right number. I hope I gave him the right number.

The next memory (and the last of the night) was of Aaron and me standing near the stage. It was late. L.A.'s hottest new DJ (and a client of Kim's father's) had just finished his last set. I was drunk and confident.

"So," I said, discreetly pulling my top down a little to show more cleavage. "Who are you supposed to be? Your costume, I mean."

"You can't tell?" he said, pretending to look hurt.

I smiled and shook my head.

"I'm Prince Charming." He took his plastic sword out of its holster.

"Oh yeah? So, who's your Cinderella?"

Aaron wrapped the sword, and his arm, around my back. "You."

The Morning After

I woke up the next morning lying under a cashmere blanket, spread out on a couch that I didn't recognize. My head was pounding, and I could barely remember a thing from the night before. There was a cup of black coffee sitting on the end table above my head.

"Drink the coffee," a tired voice told me.

I sat up and realized that I was still wearing my costume from the night before. "What happened?" I asked as I realized that the light pink room I was in was not my own.

"You got drunk." Alissa plopped down on the couch next to me.

"And you hit it off with Aaron!" Kim sat down, too.

Hit it off? I did? Really?

"Cool! Um, where's the bathroom?" My head was throbbing and waves of nausea had begun to travel up my throat. I stood up and looked around.

"Right down here," Courtney directed me. Her bedroom was a large suite, and the bathroom was within it, just behind the dressing room. I stopped Courtney at the bathroom's mirrored door.

"Did I do anything stupid?" I asked.

"No! You basically just sat with Aaron all cozy on the couches until you passed out and we carried you home."

How embarrassing. But back to this Aaron thing? "And what about Aaron? I mean, I feel bad saying this, but all I remember is that he was pretty cute. Anything else?"

"Yeah, cute . . . and smart . . . and athletic. He's the perfect catch, Becky!" She paused. "Oh, and I gave him your screen name, so you should probably be expecting an instant message one of these days!"

Courtney's stepmom was approximately the same age as Darcy, but the stepmom was a better cook. Alissa, Kim, Courtney, and I sat around the marble island in Courtney's kitchen picking at an egg-white frittata. Courtney went completely silent when her stepmom reemerged wearing nothing but a red negligee. Alissa and Kim just kept forking at their eggs, but I caught Courtney's eye, and I saw the pain. I could only imagine how awful it would be if, someday, Darcy had breakfast at our house, wearing lingerie.

We drank coffee and rehashed details from the night before, laughing at stupid things we'd done and checking our cell phones for text messages from cute boys.

The Rules

At school on Monday, the Room was abuzz with P & H gossip. I didn't run into any of the Trinity that morning, and by the time All-School Assembly came around, I was sufficiently convinced that they were avoiding me and that we weren't really friends after all. As I walked into the auditorium, I saw them sitting together. There was an empty seat beside Kim, but no one specifically beckoned me over to it, so I sat a row behind them, with Taylor.

"Hey," I said, settling into the seat. I didn't worry about asking permission to sit with her.

"Hey." Taylor tucked her legs, which were covered in heavy navy blue tights and a slightly too-long skirt, under her on the chair. "So, did you have fun at P & H?"

"Um . . ." I paused. What should I say? Taylor didn't go to the party, and moreover, she didn't really approve of everything that the party was about. I finally decided on "It was certainly interesting." That was just ambiguous enough. I didn't want to admit that it had been my best night all year. I didn't think Taylor would share my excitement at Aaron calling me his Cinderella. "So, what did you do this weekend?" I said, hoping to direct the conversation away from me.

"I helped my dad move." Taylor pulled her long braid over her shoulder. "I can't stand moving."

"Moving sucks," I agreed. "My mom found a new apartment. Again," I told Taylor. "And she wants to move in right away. I'm not looking forward to it."

"I never even got to see your last place," Taylor said.

"Well, you should come to the new place then," I told her.

"Excuse me, ladies. If I could have your attention," said Mrs. Donnelly, the head of the upper school, from the podium at the front of the room. The hall went quiet within a minute. Mrs. Donnelly didn't usually speak at assemblies—that was Ms. Morton's job. Seeing Mrs. D. up at the podium meant something serious must be happening.

I'm sure it's not in the job description, but I had rarely seen Mrs. Donnelly without a trademark article of Burberry clothing. Today, she wore a brown plaid scarf draped over a black peacoat. Her hair, as always, was curled and set to caramel-colored perfection.

"Girls. Quiet, please." She tapped at the podium. "There's an unpleasant issue that I must bring up. Your grade-level leaders are handing out papers so that you may follow along with what I'm saying. On these papers, the Whitbread School Understanding is printed."

Ugh, the Understanding. It's the social contract Whitbread sends out over the summer, and each student has to sign it and, ultimately, abide by it. The irony of the fact that our social contract was called the *Understanding* did not escape me. Because I would bet that a good portion of the school didn't quite understand it, much less abide by it.

"The Understanding, as you all know, is a very important part of our school," Mrs. Donnelly continued. "Without it, there would be no honor code and no off-campus lunch privileges, and your teachers would have to stay in the classroom while you take tests."

The auditorium was hushed. A pile of maroon handouts came my way. I took one and passed the rest along.

"You are all Whitbread girls, and whether in or out of uniform, you represent the school. Now, I have friends in the neighborhood who tell me they run into my girls on Larchmont and can't believe the way they are acting or the things they are saying," Mrs. Donnelly said.

"Fuck," I heard Alissa whisper. So maybe that rumor about Alissa doing coke in the bathroom of a boutique on Larchmont wasn't just a rumor.

"When you are out for lunch, or getting coffee after school, or at a party on a Friday night, you need to remember that you are a Whitbread girl and that all your actions reflect on the school. If your actions are unacceptable, you may be suspended or receive demerits."

A hushed murmur traveled through the room as the words "at a party on a Friday night" sank in.

"You may be expelled for such actions as, say, showing up drunk at a Stratfield dance."

I turned to Taylor, who was rebraiding her hair. "So wherever we go, Whitbread is watching us?"

"That's the way it seems," Taylor said, her eyes staring forward.

"This past weekend, many upper school students attended a party." My stomach dropped. I'd never done anything that could get me in trouble at school so the panic I felt was of an entirely new variety. I leaned forward and tapped Courtney on the back. She shrugged her shoulders. "I am told there was drinking and risqué dancing, not to mention the outfits."

Shit. Now would have been a good moment to have the ability to recall more than just four memories from that night.

"Pictures from this event were posted on facebook.com, where many of you list Whitbread as your high school. The head of another school contacted me to let me know that there were pictures, online, of some of my girls wearing very little clothing and holding red plastic cups."

Mrs. Donnelly went on about how the girls who were in the photographs had been talked to and we should take this as a lesson.

Wait—what? How had I escaped that?

I poked Courtney a little harder. She turned around and shook her head. Kim leaned back toward me and whispered, "Don't worry. We've got it covered." I could feel Taylor's eyes boring into me. I avoided turning to look at her.

That day, almost a hundred girls changed their Facebook network from Whitbread School to one of a few random California cities.

I ran into Alissa in the bathroom before AP English. She was coming out of the large stall, sniffling a little. A small plastic bag filled with a white powder was balanced on top of her poetry anthology.

"Want some?" she asked. I wondered if there were cameras in the bathrooms. It probably didn't matter, I realized. Whitbread would never expel Alissa Hargrove, especially since her father had just made a several-million-dollar donation for the new construction project.

"I'm good. Thanks, though." The truth was, I was terrified of cocaine. And I was sure that it wouldn't combine well with my various anti-anxiety medications.

"So, what happened? With the Facebook stuff, I mean."

"We took care of it."

"How? I mean, what did you do? Weren't there pictures of you on Facebook?"

"Yeah. You, too." I regretted not having checked Facebook that weekend. "But we got a tip that this shit was happening, so we took all the pictures of us offline. So don't worry, you won't get in trouble."

Us? She had said "us." I pulled a strand of highlighted hair over my ear and turned away, trying to hide the smile I knew was coming.

Moving On

*A*s it turned out, I, like Taylor, would be moving that week. Mom wanted to waste no time. The new apartment looked as though it hadn't been renovated since the mid 1970s, which was fine with Mom.

"Oh, this is great! I can add a renovation aspect to the show. I'll discuss the process of redoing my new apartment. That would be great, don't you think, Becky?" Mom had asked as we did a walk-through after school one day.

The walls in what Mom said would be my bedroom were wallpapered with fluorescent peacocks.

"I don't know."

"We'll redecorate the whole place, Becky!"

We had to. There were handicap bars in the shower. As

far as the building itself, the location was good. Doheny Park stood right at the corner of the Sunset Strip, at the edge of the Beverly Hills city limit. And apartments were for sale, not lease. There was only one unit available in the building, and it was Apartment 903, the same number as our apartment at Beach Tower. Mom took it as a sign.

She had gone into escrow and begun preparing for the renovation.

"It's perfect," Mom had gushed as we toured the kitchen. "Doheny Park is one of the hippest buildings in L.A. right now."

"And Paris Hilton just moved in. She's so hot," Jack had added.

Just who everyone wants as a neighbor.

We moved on Thursday, in the early afternoon. I was at school, and then at June Kauffman's, so once again I didn't see my new room until I got home in the evening. Mom was excited for Jack and me to see the apartment. It was still in the midst of renovations, but Mom insisted we move in anyway. Everything was in boxes, and I'd had trouble finding a skirt to wear to school that morning. I'd settled for one from the seventh grade that was still in the box of clothes I had brought from my dad's house that summer. The skirt was so short that my boxers (which were chic only at my school, I'm sure) hung out from beneath the pleated gray hem.

The only thing that was immediately set up in the new apartment was the computer and Internet connection. I was sitting in bed, researching AIDS orphans in Uganda, when I received an instant message.

It read, *New message from Playaaron.*

I knew immediately who it was.

Hey, he had typed.

Fingers shaking, I replied.

Globalgirl: *Hey.*

It was beginning to come back to me, what had happened that night. I remembered sitting with him on the couch, our legs touching. I had had to go to the bathroom but I hadn't wanted to leave him. I had been afraid that by the time I got back, he would have already lost interest. And I'd loved the feeling in the pit of my stomach—the fluttering that told me maybe, just maybe, he liked me.

Playaaron: *What's up?*

Not 2 much, I replied. I was careful to insert a *2* instead of *too*. On the Internet, for reasons beyond my understanding, it was cool to abbreviate and misspell. Aaron responded after only a few seconds, informing me that he was watching the baseball game and playing online poker. Each time my computer beeped with the NEW MESSAGE notification, I got a little thrill. I wanted to see him again.

Globalgirl: *So, how's ur week going so far?*

I tried to give him a good opportunity to ask if I wanted to hang out. I didn't know much about boys, but I did know they were the ones who were supposed to do the asking. Instead, he told me about soccer practice and how his coach had been a total dick to the team.

I stared at the screen and the dark blue writing and the soccer ball icon and without remembering to think, I pressed ENTER, sending him the sentence I wished he would type.

Globalgirl: *What are you doing this weekend?*

Playaaron: *No plans yet. . . .*

I wrung my hands together to keep myself from typing any more. I waited to see if he would continue. And then, I just didn't want to wait any more. *Do you want to maybe hang out or something?* I wrote in the blank box. And then—by mistake again, of course—I sent it. I knew that the boy was supposed to do the asking out. That was the way it worked in the books I read, at least. But I was a feminist. I didn't have to wait for the boy to ask me. And besides, I didn't have the patience for that.

I stood up and walked in a circle around my bedroom, not wanting to wait while he typed, and not wanting to see him say no. The blue writing popped up on the screen: *Yeah, we could see a movie or something.* That same shiver I had felt the night of P & H went flying up my arms.

Okay, I replied. *That sounds good.*

Even though I had done the asking, that didn't change the fact that it was a date. Right?

What to Wear

"I'm going out with this boy I met at P & H," I told Amanda on the phone the Saturday afternoon of my date with Aaron.

"A date! With who?" But before I could answer, Amanda had continued with, "I have news, too. At my dad's opening last night, I hooked up with this actor from the play." This was a new Amanda entirely. Old Amanda never talked about hooking up like it was as casual as going out to lunch. It seemed like she was becoming an entirely different person. Then again, maybe I was, too.

But even though I seemed to be making an unlikely transformation into a popular, dateable girl, I hadn't gained any fashion sense. I had no idea what might be an appropriate first-date outfit.

"I'm leaving soon," I told my dad that afternoon. It was the end of my week with him, and I hadn't spent more than five minutes at a time with him.

"Where are you going?" he asked, eyes glued to the computer screen. "Over to Mom's?"

"No, I have plans." A date, I reminded myself. I had a date. But somehow, the thought of telling my dad I had a date seemed too weird for words.

"I just have to finish reading this one brief and then I'll be right with you. Wait just a sec, okay, honey?"

No, not okay. I walked down the hallway in a huff. This was one of those moments I talked with June about. According to June, I'm supposed to remind myself that I don't need him. I want my dad's attention, and I love my dad, but I am a complete person with or without him. And I don't need anyone else's validation to be a great person.

That's what June Kauffman says I am. Sometimes she switches it up and calls me gifted, and when she does that, I say that maybe she's overestimating me. But she says she's not.

I slammed my bedroom door shut, hoping the noise would startle my dad. When I got no response, I continued into the dressing room, flipping on the light switch as I walked. Sliding open the door to my closet, I began to tear through clothes, tossing onto the floor in front of me any shirts and skirts that I thought might work.

Finally, I had a pile of tank tops, polo shirts, jeans, and

sweaters lying in front of me. And none of it would do. I wanted to look casual, but not grungy; sophisticated, but not as if I were trying too hard. I wanted to be Alissa Hargrove, who had a personal stylist, or Courtney Gross, whose closet was full of clothes because her stepmother couldn't ever pass up a designer sale.

My outfit problems, I decided, could be boiled down to Whitbread. During the school year, I get it in my head that all articles of clothing I purchase should be either navy blue or white, because that's what I wear five days a week. The idea that I might need clothes to wear on the weekends always manages to escape me; I'm too busy trying to buy the right clothes to make my uniform look effortlessly chic with a tinge of I-just-rolled-out-of-bed.

So, I had plenty of navy sweatshirts, but for a date, that wouldn't work. I dug a black V-neck out of the pile and stood up, holding it to my chest and staring in the mirror. The front was cut deep enough to create the illusion of cleavage, but was showing my nonexistent cleavage on a first date too risqué? I didn't want to seem like I was asking for it.

I pulled on my skinniest jeans and tugged a cable-knit sweater over my head. Finishing the look with some ankle boots I had taken from my mom a while back, I decided I was ready.

And, with perfect timing, that was exactly when my phone rang. I ran out of the dressing room and into my bedroom to answer. "Hello?"

"Honey, hi, it's Mom. Where are you?"

"Dad's. Just getting ready."

"You're going out with that boy tonight! I forgot. Why don't you stop here on your way out? I could help you get dressed."

My mom would seem to be the perfect personal stylist, but knowing her, she might go overboard. I wasn't sure how to graciously decline my mother's clothing advice, and I didn't want to meet Aaron at the movie theater wearing a sequined top or diamond necklace.

"I just featured this great new designer on my show. She makes super-comfy dresses. I brought a few home; you could wear one tonight."

"I don't know. . . ."

"Just check them out. This designer was telling me that her stuff is all the rage with girls your age. She's been featured in *People* three times this month." As stupid as I knew that was, I was sold.

And, as it turned out, the dress actually was perfect. Mom dug a pearl necklace out of one of the moving boxes, but I declined. I accepted the offer of lip gloss and gave myself a once-over in the lobby mirror as I waited for the valet to bring my car to the front.

The black dress fit snugly enough to be flattering but not so tight as to look slutty. I had changed into flats because, as my mom reminded me, I was going to be doing enough walking around that I wouldn't be comfortable in heels.

With the finishing touches of mascara and more peachy lip gloss, I set off.

It was rush hour, which was a good thing for me because I was running early. The Grove, my destination, is one of those slightly ridiculous Los Angeles locations. It's an outdoor space that was designed with some sort of Tuscan theme in mind. At least it has a fresh vibe and better ambience than the nearby indoor mall, the Beverly Center. The Grove's buildings are a distressed cream color with intricate tiling on the roof, and a two-story trolley travels down the "cobbled" streets, picking up shoppers at one end of the mall and depositing them at the other. All told, the trolley trip takes about three minutes. It would be shorter, but the driver makes a few stops to extend the experience. In the middle of the central courtyard, there's a large pond where fountains spurt water high into the air. My mom and I went to the Grove the day it opened. An outside mall on our side of town was a big deal. Plus, Nordstrom was having a sale.

As I took the elevator down from the parking structure, I stared into the sliver of mirror and tried to examine and assess my reflection.

I just hoped that I looked good enough.

Aaron was standing on the bridge that crossed over the fountain, leaning back against one of the rails. His hair was just as shaggy and unkempt as I remembered, and he wore a white T-shirt with baggy khaki shorts. He smiled when he saw me.

"Hey," I said, unsure of how to act with a boy I had spent a whole evening with (even though I couldn't remember it all).

"Hey back," he said, beginning to walk with me across the bridge and toward the new luxury movie theater.

"So, how was the rest of your week?" I asked.

"It was fine." He shrugged. "What movie do you want to see?"

We were standing beneath a large marquee right inside the movie theater's vault-ceilinged lobby. "I don't know. What do you want to see?" I had become attuned to the fact that picking a movie was apparently a point of contention between couples.

"You pick," Aaron told me, flashing a smile.

So I picked the historical romantic comedy that was supposed to, surprisingly, have important political undertones.

"Two tickets for *Henry*," Aaron told the woman behind the marble-top counter, removing a square black wallet from his back pocket.

Was he going to pay? Was I supposed to offer to pay? The woman behind the counter gave me a wink, and I suddenly felt very uncomfortable. It must have been clear that we were two teenagers on a date. If I turned around I would probably find some older couple looking at us and whispering, "How cute."

So I didn't turn around. And I let him buy the tickets.

After a stop at the concession stand, we walked down the hall and into Theater 12. And, in the darkness, standing in the aisle, I felt my stomach flutter once again.

"So, where should we sit?" he asked. This was a question with meaning, I knew. If we sat closer to the front, it meant we were really going to see the movie, but if we sat closer to the back . . . well, maybe movie-viewing wouldn't be the only activity going on.

All of a sudden I felt a little like an adult and a lot more like a child, all at the same time.

"I picked the movie," I told Aaron, whispering beneath the coming attractions. "You pick where we sit." I followed Aaron to the right side of the theater, and then down the aisle as we headed toward the back. He stopped a few rows from the back wall.

"This good?" he whispered.

Heart racing, I nodded.

I could barely concentrate on the movie and almost failed to catch the major plot points because I was so aware of Aaron sitting right next to me, Aaron sharing my armrest, Aaron offering me popcorn. I accepted the popcorn, leaning over him to reach the bucket. He smelled fresh, like aftershave. My arm brushed his as I reached over, and a little electric shock shot up my body. I allowed my right arm to dangle over the armrest. His hand was on his knee, just inches beneath my fingers. The movie was almost over and I was staring at the screen, when I saw his hand move up just the slightest amount, and suddenly, his fingers were interlaced with mine. I closed my fingers down on his hesitantly, unsure whether I should look at him and smile, like I wanted to, or continue focusing on the movie. I watched the king of England dance around a ballroom for a few minutes. Aaron had begun to stroke my hand with his thumb, and I couldn't believe what was happening.

Then, when the credits were about to roll, he kissed me. I don't remember how it happened exactly, but I remember turning in to face him, and him leaning forward, and it was then that my heart started pounding. My lips met his, tentatively, and all I can remember thinking was *Shit. My breath must smell like popcorn.*

Just one day later, I thought back on the evening and realized I couldn't remember what it had felt like to be kissed. All I knew was that I wanted to do it again. The night before hadn't ended at that first kiss. The first kiss had turned into a second, and then Aaron stuck his tongue in my mouth and I realized just how awkward, and not particularly sexy, making out was. The idea of it was better than the act itself. I had to spend most of my time trying to figure out what to do with my tongue and where to put my hands, one of which was trapped underneath my leg, squished between the armrest and my body.

Oh, and then there was the issue of being in a public

movie theater. It wasn't at all how I imagined my first kiss (sunset at the beach), but aside from occasional nervous glances toward the rows in front of us, I was content.

That night, I wrote in my old diary for the first time in a long time. *Diary*, I wrote, *I finally feel like a normal teenage girl.*

Friends Like These

"So, are you really dating that Stratfield guy?" Taylor asked me in Advisory on Monday morning. Taylor had asked me about my weekend, and I, reluctantly, had told her about Aaron.

I had also told the Trinity about my date, but only Courtney knew that Aaron had been my first kiss. With Alissa and Kim, I had tried to act as if it were no big deal. I was nervous about telling Taylor—nervous that, for whatever reason, she wouldn't approve.

"Well, I mean, we went on *a* date. I don't know if that means we're dating." I couldn't help getting excited about the prospect, though.

"Well, um, congratulations, I guess."

* * *

The next week, at the next Model UN meeting, I announced our committee assignments. The upcoming conference in Berkeley was a team delegate conference, which meant that each delegation was composed of two people.

"I'm really excited about this," I told the girls sitting in the desks in front of me. The room was so crowded that a few sat on the floor. I couldn't help being impressed with myself. Club turnout had increased—and I hadn't needed Amanda to do any recruiting. She had said she would—that if I needed help she would send out messages to Whitbread girls, even though she no longer was one.

I had declined her offer for help. Finally, I had enough confidence in myself and in my club to post flyers around school advertising the club and suggesting that girls join. And join they did.

More and more girls had started coming to MUN meetings recently, ever since the flyers . . . ever since Aaron. And, even more important, some of them were actually interested in international affairs. One ninth-grade girl even came up to me after a meeting, asking if she might be able to research the militarization of space. She was really interested in that topic, she told me.

Mr. Elwright was busy fumbling with some maps over the whiteboard, desperately trying to pull down the one that showed Africa. Every time he pulled one map down, another clicked open, and he had trouble rolling both back into place. It was like a scene out of a sitcom.

"As you all know, Whitbread MUN isn't just about debating issues. We're going to actually make a difference." I was so glad we had been assigned Uganda. Mr. E. had warned me we might get some nation like Canada.

How boring.

I gave a glance toward the Trinity. Courtney was smiling, Kim's face was entirely blank, and Alissa was nodding along with my words. They had made it to the meeting on time that day, for once.

"I've done a little background on the issues plaguing Uganda. AIDS orphans are a major problem, as is clean water supply."

Kim raised her hand. Her eyebrows were scrunched together, and the hand that wasn't raised was busy twirling a strand of long, highlighted hair. "Wait, shouldn't they have plenty clean water? You know, because of . . ." Her voice faltered.

I pursed my lips together and gave a glance back at the large map of Africa that Mr. E. had finally managed to pull down. A surplus of clean water in Uganda? "No, um, why?" I asked.

Courtney whispered something into Kim's ear, and Kim's hand shot in the air once more. "Duh!" she said. "Because of the Niagara Falls!"

Taylor dropped the fork from her mouth and started to laugh. Alissa turned around and gave a harsh look to Taylor.

I was trying to stifle laughter myself. It wasn't proper to laugh at someone, I knew. And it certainly wouldn't win me any friends either. "Niagara Falls?" I asked, a chuckle escaping from my mouth. I tried to disguise it as a cough and glanced toward Mr. E. His lips were tight in a grimace.

"Obviously. There's tons of water there."

I spoke before thinking. "Yeah, there is plenty of water at Niagara Falls. But we're not representing America." My tone was probably cutting, and Taylor broke into another round of almost-silent laughter.

Kim and Courtney had no idea what was going on. Alissa butted in, "It was just a joke! I didn't know diplomats had no sense of humor." Turning around in her chair, she winked at Taylor. I wondered for a second if that wink was meant to be friendly. Then, I found myself being glad that the wink and the narrow-eyed look hadn't been directed at me.

It clearly hadn't been a joke, but I didn't want to pursue the issue any further. The mother of one of the girls in the room was a well-known celebrity gossip columnist. And I didn't want it getting out that I had gotten in an argument with Alissa Hargrove (over geography, no less!). Especially since we had just become friends. Even if Taylor kept shooting me questioning looks from her spot in the back row.

At the end of the meeting, I was at the podium, organizing my papers. You can take the depression out of a girl, but the OCD will never go away. Taylor approached me on her way out.

"You know, you're not as Hollywoodified as I thought," she said. This coming from an aspiring actress who was the daughter of an Academy Award–winning costume designer. Of course, it was true that she didn't lower herself to jumping through any Whitbread social hoops.

Unlike, well, me.

"Your eyes really lit up when you started talking about Uganda. You're not one of them. You're better than that." Taylor gestured to the Trinity, who were sitting on a bench outside the classroom, waiting for me.

I hoped I was better, that I would never place so much importance on a sample sale or a movie premiere, but I still wanted to fit in. To be *one of them*. I was tired of being the weird Smart Girl.

But was Taylor criticizing me and my social decisions?

Kim rolled her eyes and beckoned me from the door.

"The three bimbos are calling you," Taylor said, turning to shoot a look at the Trinity.

"Hey! Just because you're jealous doesn't mean you have to be obnoxious." I gathered my papers and left the room in a huff. As I walked to class with the Trinity, Alissa said, "Taylor thinks she's better than everyone. News flash—she's not."

"I know! She's so annoying," I lashed out, still feeling the sting of Taylor's words. "And get this," I added, "she thinks we're actually friends."

Alissa laughed. "As if you'd ever be friends with her. You're so much cooler than her."

I was cool. Alissa Hargrove said that *I* was cool. I had gone out with an extremely attractive, very popular boy, and I was friends with the most popular girls in school. Life was good.

Doheny Park
Is a Popular Place to Be

"**Y**ou live *here?*" Taylor said in a tone of what sounded like disgust. Her nose was wrinkled up as she grabbed her reusable water bottle and tote bag from the passenger side of her car.

She had approached me in the parking lot that morning and reminded me that I'd invited her over to our new apartment. This was supposed to be our first week living there, but because Mom had been so eager to move, we had now been at Doheny Park for a few weeks already.

"Yeah," I'd said, not wanting to uninvite her, and feeling guilty about making fun of her earlier that week.

"What's wrong with living here?" I asked defensively now, as we got ready to leave our cars in the large circular driveway. Aside from the fact that everything was still in boxes and the hip new director across the hall who had decided to gut his apartment always had a team of workers shuffling in and out, everything was basically fine. But who was Taylor to judge?

"Nothing," she said quickly. "Nothing's wrong with living here." Even so, I could see her spine straighten, and she gripped her water bottle tightly. I pulled my skirt down a little and lifted my laptop case out of the car.

I very quickly found out what the problem was. For Taylor, I mean. When we entered the lobby, there were two men in workout clothes sitting on one of the couches. One of the men was tall, thin, and Hispanic. The other was a little shorter and a little pudgier, and had a head of curly blond hair. The blond one locked eyes with Taylor, who suddenly said, "Let's go. Now." She dashed toward the wall of elevators, her long sweater flapping behind her.

"Taylor?"

"Bruce." Taylor turned around slowly and spoke flatly.

"Lucas, it's Taylor! Taylor, what are you doing here?" The blond man stood up and took a step toward Taylor. I immediately saw the resemblance.

"Is that . . ." I began. Then I saw the pain in Taylor's face and stopped. And then I saw Lucas put his arm around Bruce, and I finally understood.

"I'm here with my friend Becky." Taylor stayed at a

distance and pushed the UP button on the elevator control panel. "She lives here, too."

The elevator opened. A man in a maroon suit emerged from behind the concierge desk and held the door open. "Mr. Tremaine?" he said. "I've just heard back from maintenance. The steam room is open now, so feel free to go on up." I could almost see a green tinge appearing in Taylor's face.

Later, in my new room, we lay on the floor researching the social stigmas against AIDS orphans in Africa. "I didn't know," I ventured.

She gave me a confused look at first, not understanding what I was talking about. But then she got it. "Yeah, I mean, I'm not trying to keep it a secret or anything." Taylor said, doodling a tree on a legal pad. "He's only been out for a month."

I tried to think of something appropriate to say.

"It's not a secret or anything," she went on. "But do you think you could . . . not tell people about it? Girls talk. I don't want the new buzz at school to be about this. Especially not the you-know-who. I mean, I know they're your friends, but . . ." She trailed off.

I nodded. The Trinity *were* my friends, and because of that, I knew what gossips they could be. "Of course not."

My words from earlier that week rushed back at me, biting me in the ass. *She thinks we're actually friends.*

Pushing those thoughts away, I turned my head toward Taylor and opened my mouth into what I hoped was a sympathetic smile. "What are friends for, right?" Her eyes were glassy. A cliché just wasn't going to cut it. "Besides, every family has its own shit to deal with."

I tried to laugh, but there wasn't really anything to laugh about.

So This Is Love

*A*aron and I were sitting in the back of an almost-empty movie theater in Westwood on our three-week anniversary, seeing the nine o'clock showing of a new animated movie. He bought the tickets, and we made out for almost the entire two hours.

"Aaron," I whispered. My breathing came in bursts as I tried to draw myself away from him. "What are we?"

Everyone at school believed that I had a new boyfriend. Except me.

Aaron sat back in his chair and looked me in the eye. His hair stuck up and his cheeks were flushed. He smiled and I shivered a little. "All I know is that you're my girlfriend, and I love you."

So not what I was expecting.

"Thanks." I said, immediately realizing that this was the wrong response. "I mean," I gripped the handle of the armrest to my right, the one farthest from Aaron. "I really appreciate it—that you feel that way." I grimaced. Why did I sound like an awkward forty-year-old?

I leaned in to kiss him before he could ask if I felt the same way.

For a fleeting moment, I found myself feeling nervous about Aaron's proclamation of love, but that feeling quickly went away. The idea that someone loved me— liked me, even—was overwhelming. Even my parents, who I knew loved me, sometimes got so busy that they didn't call to check in or show up for dinner. Not Aaron. Aaron called when he said he would and texted me daily. And I called and texted back. He made me feel special.

The night after he told me he loved me, Aaron opened our phone conversation by saying, "So, I'm on Facebook right now, and you know the thing where you say who you're in a relationship with? I don't know, but I was just updating my profile, and . . ."

"Put me down!" I tried to sound casual and not too eager, but my heart was racing. Saying he loved me was one thing, but changing a Facebook relationship status meant that this relationship was *really* official. That Aaron was proud of me and wanted me to be listed at the top of his profile page.

"Okay, cool."

"So, see you Friday?" I stretched my legs out in front of me.

"Can't wait."

"Me either," I half whispered before ending the call and picking up my book.

When my parents told me they were getting divorced, I was convinced that I would never be happy again.

But all of a sudden, I wasn't sad anymore. Some of that might have been my new medications—I'd even stopped realphabetizing my books every day—but I thought that most of it had to do with Aaron. I certainly wasn't happy because of my parents, since they were just as crazy as ever. And my newfound popularity was definitely great, but it only increased my anxieties. I had started spending an extra half hour in the morning getting ready, worried that if my uniform wasn't just right, if my hair was frizzy, or if a zit was showing, the Trinity would remember that I, Becky Miller, wasn't actually cool. No, it had to be Aaron. Because whenever I thought about Aaron, my stomach fluttered, and I realized that I must be cool enough because cooler-than-cool Aaron Winters liked me—had chosen me.

And then, because nobody was there to tell me that I was being immature, I tossed *Heart of Darkness* aside for a moment, stood up on my floral-print sheets, and jumped up and down, the coils squeaking and my head almost touching the ceiling, until I finally fell back on the pillows, smiling with exhaustion and, dare I say it, happiness.

When It Rains, It Pours

*I*t is a myth that it never rains in Los Angeles, because it does.

But it wasn't supposed to rain inside.

Mom had an HWPC meeting one Sunday morning, and as all the women gathered in the living room, talking over one another in attempts to get a word in edgewise, I pulled the blankets over my head, hoping to get another hour or two of sleep. I might have gone out to the living room to listen in on the meeting, except that it was only nine in the morning and I really couldn't get my mind around the idea of getting out of bed, much less putting on clothes.

It was hard to get back to sleep, though. The women

talked loudly. I overheard Laura Turner introducing my mom to someone, and throughout the course of the conversation, I realized that the "someone" was Courtney's stepmother, Marisa, who had come along to the meeting with Laura and was "so excited to meet Becky's mother!" But Courtney didn't really like Marisa, so I felt no need to hop out of bed, put on my game face, and go say hello. Instead I tucked a pillow over my head and tried to get some sleep.

Two hours later, I was standing on the balcony, staring through the glass door at my bedroom, my hands on my Mickey Mouse pajama–clad hips. I had woken up when a drop of water landed on my forehead. Sitting straight up in my twin bed, I'd stared at the ceiling. Suddenly, water had plopped onto the pillow to my left, leaving a dark, circular mark. Then there had been another drop, right on top of my head. "Mom! It's . . . raining," I'd called out, still sitting upright and unnerved in bed.

I'd had no idea what time it was, but I'd figured that the HWPC meeting must have been over because the apartment was quiet.

"No it's not; don't be silly. Look, it's a beautiful day out!" Mom had responded from the living room.

And then, as if on cue, a steady splash of water had come streaming down from the ceiling onto my bright white carpet and trickled along the wall closest to my bathroom. "Mom! I think you should come see this."

"Mommy, what's going on?" Jack's voice had rung out.

I had curled into a ball at the top of my bed. The carpet was soaking up the water that had fallen from above, but then there was more, trickling down the pale yellow corner walls of my bedroom and falling in steady "plinks" into a growing puddle in the center of the room.

"Mom! I'm sitting on the toilet and I'm scared to get up! And since when does it rain inside? Is this water? It's all over the bathroom, Mom!" a frantic Jack shouted. Then, "Shit, Mom! It's raining pee!"

I heard Mom's heels clicking as she passed my bedroom and stopped at the entrance to her bathroom suite. "Oh, great," Mom sighed. "Becky, if you thought that it was raining in your room, you should check this out. Jack, come out of there! I have to call the super to get him to turn the water off!"

The espadrilles that I had worn the previous day were sitting by my bed, so even though they weren't very practical, I had put them on and ventured toward the hallway. Mom was right; her bathroom was completely flooded; the carpets were soggy, paint was coming off the molding, and there was water dripping down in several different places.

"Jack, come out of the bathroom. It's not *that* scary. And it's not pee. The building manager should be here any second."

Jack had showed up behind me wearing boxer shorts, a T-shirt, and a look of disbelief.

"It's not wet in the living room, so why don't you two go sit in there while we wait for the manager to come and turn off the water valve. I'll go try to find some buckets to put down."

Ten minutes later, the doorbell rang. As Mom went to answer it, she'd turned to Jack and me and said, "This is when you're glad you live in a full-service building."

Yes, unless you happened to be standing there looking like a complete fool in flannel pajamas and espadrilles.

A man dressed in a gray suit was standing at the front door.

"Ms. Miller, I think that we have identified the problem," the man said, holding a walkie-talkie to his ear. We believe that a pipe has burst in the bathroom of the apartment above yours."

"Bathroom?" Jack squealed, jumping up. "Mom, I told you!"

"It's just water . . . right?"

"Just water, yes."

"So how do we get it to stop? Is there a water valve or something?"

The building manager secured the walkie-talkie at his hip using the clip. "Unfortunately, Ms. Miller, only our super knows where the water control valve is, and . . . he's not in right now."

Doheny Park prided itself on having a twenty-four-hour live-in super. Who, I guess, just wasn't living-in at the moment.

For the next few hours, several more employees entered our apartment, and a building-wide search for the water valve ensued. It was a futile search, and the whole time, water continued to drip into our apartment, where we hoped it was landing only in the buckets and mixing bowls that had been placed on the floor. By the time the super got back (he claimed he'd been visiting his sick mother and had forgotten to turn on his cell) and the water was shut off, plenty of damage had been done. Walls and floors were wet, soggy carpets needed to be torn up, and wires were hanging everywhere—the apartment looked like a disaster zone.

Mom sent us to Dad's house that night. She said that by the time we came back to her, everything would be figured out. I didn't want to leave her. In its current state, the apartment was not somewhere that one would want to live in, especially alone. But Mom insisted, claiming that her bedroom hadn't really been harmed, so she should be fine for a day or two. She could use the bathroom in the building's gym, she assured us.

I lay in my bed at my dad's house that night, unable to get to sleep. I had to sleep; I had school the next day. But I couldn't close my eyes for long enough to give in to the powers of REM. I got out of bed and reorganized my books by page count, thickest to thinnest, trying to ignore the feeling that this had happened because things had been going well for me, that after my several-week high, this was the inevitable fall.

Home Sweet Home (Take Two)

I was in math when Mrs. Donnelly's assistant interrupted the class. "Excuse me, I have a note for Becky Miller," she said. She handed me a folded piece of Whitbread stationery.

"What's the note about?" Alissa leaned over and whispered.

I shook my head and shrugged my shoulders. I smiled nervously up at the teacher and unfolded the sheet of paper.

It read:

I've been fighting with the insurance company about where we're moving to. Talked with Laura, and we've got it settled. Get what you want from the apartment and meet me at the Four Seasons after school.

I assumed she meant Laura Turner, who was well known as a vicious attorney.

"I think," I whispered to Alissa, "I might be moving into the Four Seasons."

I waited to gauge her response. "Cool," she said. "Caroline Parkman's living there right now, too. What did you get for number 27?" She spoke as if living in the Four Seasons was the most normal thing in the world.

Perfectly normal chaos.

Jack, I realized when I got back to Doheny Park that day, hadn't received a note from Mom; I guess I was responsible for giving him the news. "Why should I believe you? As far as I know, you're just randomly saying that we're going to move out of our apartment and into the fucking Four Seasons?" he asked, sliding his finger around his iPod dial to pump up the volume. But he did believe me, it seemed, because he grabbed a suitcase from the hall closet and began to stuff it with hats and video games.

Walking into my bedroom, or what remained of it, I couldn't figure out what to pack. Was I *moving* to the Four Seasons? Was this a *vacation?* We had two big suitcases stored on the top shelf of the hall closet, and these might have been plenty for both of us, except that when I tried to add books and Jack tried to stuff in his Xbox 360, we ran out of room. So, cramming whatever wouldn't fit in the suitcases into tote bags and backpacks, we created a pile in the front hall, right behind the huge industrial vacuums that had been brought in as part of the failed cleanup process.

An hour later, I felt fairly confident in saying that walking into the Beverly Hills Four Seasons in my school uniform, carrying backpacks and duffel bags and dragging along a Game Boy–playing little brother, was not one of my classiest moments.

Oh, yeah, and while I was explaining who I was to the concierge, Jack, who was wearing a sweatshirt with "J-Zizzy" emblazoned across the front—a step up from his Halloween costume—was chatting it up with Jay-Z, who was standing behind us in line. "Dude, I like your sweatshirt," I heard Jay-Z say.

I told the woman standing at the desk that I was there to check in, and no, I wasn't Kathy Miller, but I was her daughter, and she would be there later.

"Ah, yes, your mother's assistant called earlier today and said that you would be coming. If you would just give Horatio your bags, he'll bring them up to your rooms for you. Eliza will show you the way."

The two-bedroom suite overlooked the hotel's circular entranceway and Doheny Drive. Sitting on top of the coffee table were bowls of M&M'S and champagne. There was a master bedroom with a king-sized bed and heavy drapes. and connected to that was a living room that had a pullout sofa, a refrigerator, a small dining table, and a coffee table. The room next door had two twin beds and a marble-top desk with a large television armoire to the right. Jack and I had to share a room? We hadn't done that since, well, never.

Mom came home that afternoon carrying a tote bag full of clothes on one shoulder and a cream-colored suit over the other. She was talking on a cell phone propped up only by her shoulder. "My apartment is currently an unacceptable living situation, and you are required to provide me and my children with comparable arrangements. Yes, I have already moved out. Well, there are other families from my children's schools currently living at the Beverly Hills Hotel because of mold, so I have made the decision, based on legal counsel, to move to a hotel that is of a comparable living situation to Doheny Park. I've moved to the Four Seasons." Mom took a breath and sat down on the couch, smiling hello. "So you'll pay for our living and food expenses until the apartment becomes inhabitable. Thank you. Good-bye." She clicked the phone shut.

"Did they agree?" I asked Mom, sitting down next to her on the couch.

"I certainly hope so."

They did agree, in the end. They, the insurance agency, would pay for our exorbitantly expensive two-bedroom suite and for every meal, no matter what or how much we ordered.

I had never really considered the possibility of living in a hotel. After all, why would I? Hotels weren't places that people lived, normally. Well, except for Eloise, who I had definitely enjoyed reading about when I was younger. And Caroline Parkman, too, apparently. But Caroline Parkman was a too-cool-for-school senior who I barely knew. And Eloise was six. She lived in the Plaza, and the book never showed how she might have to remember to order her breakfast the night before or put away her books and papers because otherwise the maid would hide them somewhere.

MUN Is M-I-N-E

Everything in MUN was going great. I had chosen my committee for the conference at Berkeley as well as the club's cause for the year. I knew Taylor would be a better teammate, but I chose Courtney as my partner. She seemed genuinely pleased. And best of all, we had begun fundraising to build a school for AIDS orphans in Uganda.

At the next club meeting, girls split up into their pairs, with each pair researching Uganda's stance on the topics of its committee. Mine was AIDS in Africa. I was thrilled that all the research I had done regarding the AIDS orphan school could be put to use in my committee sessions. Courtney was sitting in the desk across from mine; we had rearranged the desks into pairs. She was researching AIDS awareness education and how Uganda felt about it.

When my cell phone vibrated against my leg telling me I had a new text message, I reached discreetly into the pocket of my skirt. Cell phone use wasn't exactly allowed during school hours. The message was from Joey: *I got South Africa!*

Joey was so sweet that I couldn't help but smile. He knew that I had Uganda, so he probably assumed we could sign on to some resolutions together.

Stratfield was coming to the conference, too, and everyone wanted to arrange a dinner for our teams, mainly because their team had boys on it. Mr. Elwright and I had convinced everyone to research first, talk about dinner later.

I text messaged Joey back, asking who his partner was. I received an almost immediate response.

Your boyfriend.

My fingers started shaking. Aaron wasn't in MUN. Had he joined just because of me? What was going on?

"What's up?" Courtney asked me.

"Nothing." I dropped the phone back into my pocket and opened up my three-ring binder. "So, have you found any statistics?"

"Becky," Mr. E. called from his desk, "do you want to give everyone an update on the school?"

"Um, sure." I stood up and walked to the front of the room. "Hey," I called out, and the room went silent apart from the shuffling of papers. All eyes were on me. "So, yesterday, I received a letter back from Namaya Hellen, my new pen pal in Uganda." I had memorized what she'd said to me. The words had stuck out, every sentence piercing me. "Both of Namaya's parents died of AIDS, and she is the sole caretaker for her three younger siblings. Namaya is only fourteen, younger than most of us. I told her about how we were raising money to help build a school for her to go to, and this is what she wrote in response: 'I am so happy you are giving us a school for orphans. Now we can learn and be like the other children.' We are making a difference, child by child."

Girls started clapping.

"We're so cool," Courtney said, daring to speak up in the full room.

That evening, I plopped down on my new bed in my new bedroom and dialed Aaron. "Hey. So I found out from Joey that you do MUN. Why didn't *you* tell me?" I asked, trying to hide the hurt I was feeling.

"Yeah, I sort of do MUN sometimes. It's not really a big deal, though."

Not a big deal? "You know how important MUN is to me," I told him.

"Yeah, but it's just a game."

I shoved my hand into a pillow. "It's not a game to me."

"I get it, I get it. Don't get worked up about it." I heard rustling on the other end of the line. "I have to finish my homework."

"Oh, okay," I said.

What I wanted to say was, "What the hell?"

Control

"**Y**ou're jumpy," June told me one Thursday afternoon. I'd been stressing about the MUN conference in Berkeley, which was only a couple weeks away. Plus, living at the Four Seasons was weird. And Dad had been spending more time with Darcy while Mom was spending more time yelling at the insurance company.

"No kidding," I said, my leg shaking.

I tilted my head up. Her eyes were waiting.

"I have a boyfriend," I said. I averted my eyes. This was my first time mentioning Aaron to June. I didn't quite understand why I had been so secretive.

"What's his name?"

"Aaron."

"Where does he go to school?"

"Stratfield."

"How long have you been going out?"

"About a month."

June seemed taken aback. "Really? So why do you think you're only telling me now?"

"I don't know." I think maybe I was afraid that telling June might somehow burst the bubble, destroy what I saw as a near-perfect relationship with Aaron (in spite of his MUN comment).

"How often do you see him?" June asked.

I put my hands underneath my thighs so that I wouldn't rip off my fingernails (one of my more annoying nervous habits). "Every weekend, I guess."

"You know what I think?"

No, I didn't know. And I wasn't sure that I wanted to.

"I think you have trouble opening up emotionally to people."

"What do you mean?" I asked.

"It all has to do with your issue with control." Which we talked about all the time. "Which is also related to your fear of being vulnerable."

I crossed my arms over my chest. Talking about feeling vulnerable made me feel vulnerable, naked almost, and I hated it. In telling June about Aaron, I had given up a part of myself, and I wanted it back.

"You feel as though you're the only one who can be counted on to protect you. It's a coping mechanism,

Becky. You close yourself off to people because you don't want to be hurt by them. And, if you don't open yourself up to others, you think that you can maintain control over whatever situation you're in. And, as you and I both know, you have been placed in many situations that you have seemingly no control over."

I thought about the divorce, about Sara Elder overmedicating me, about Darcy in her too-short skirts, and about Doheny Park filling with water. I thought about the time when I was in third grade and Grandma called me fat, and how I had spent the next few months refusing to eat anything with a calorie count over one hundred. And about when I was ten and Dad's dad had died and Mom was out of town, and Dad got frighteningly drunk and I tried to take care of him and make dinner for Jack. How I forgot to go to the bathroom until late in the afternoon the next day, when Mom came home, because I was so concerned with keeping everything, and everyone, together.

"What do you mean?" I asked, nervous.

"You must see it. As a way of dealing with situations, you detach yourself and keep the real you bottled up inside, somewhere you hope it will be safe."

I couldn't think of any good response because on some level, I knew that it was true. I wanted to tell Aaron I loved him, but I was scared. I was scared of attaching emotion to situations; I spoke about them, wrote about them, lived through them in a clinical fashion, as if I were a reporter covering a story. Except in this case, it was the story of my life.

And I couldn't stay on the ceiling forever, acting as a bird's-eye-view observer of my own story. Someday—someday soon, maybe—I'd have to turn off the MUTE button and unplug the TiVo. It would be time to start living inside myself.

"You understand what I'm saying, don't you?" June said. It was less a question than a statement.

"Yeah," I told her. "I think I do. But what am I supposed to do about it?"

"Try to think more simply some of the time. Concentrate on being in the moment and focusing on what's going on around you, and try to let that be enough. Look for good things and think about what things make you feel good." I thought about my Bright Side Lists. I had never done very well with those.

Concentrate on being in the moment. Okay, I could try.

Celebration

*T*he Doheny Park apartment was going to take months to fix, but hotel life, despite the many amenities, was becoming stifling. So Mom had started looking at houses to rent. Before we moved out, though, I was going to have a party.

My mom was proud of my psychological state of well-being and wanted me to celebrate, so she said I could throw a party. And what venue could possibly be better than the Beverly Hills Four Seasons?

I was struck by the weirdness of the whole situation. I was being congratulated for not being mentally unstable. For most people, mental stability isn't something that warrants congratulations.

On Wednesday night, I went out to dinner with Alissa,

Kim, Courtney, and Aaron to plan my party. I'd told them it was one of the perks of Divorce Guilt, not a celebration of my sanity. It was a school night, but Alissa's dad's friend had just opened a brand-new Greek fusion restaurant in West L.A., and as Alissa explained, we simply had to check it out. The owner had informed his waitstaff and maître d' that we—a group of very important young people—were coming, and that we ought to be properly taken care of.

"It needs to be small. Not a party even, really. A kick-back would be fine," I explained to everyone at the table. "Maybe even just us?"

Courtney whispered something to Alissa, who subsequently lit up and said, "How about this Friday? Come on, Becky!"

I sat next to Aaron in the booth. Beneath the table, he was holding my hand. This Friday? Aaron and I had been planning on doing a movie night at Aaron's house, in his family's new screening room. I raised my eyebrows. I wanted to have the party, but I didn't want Aaron to think I was blowing off our date. He squeezed my hand a little tighter and whispered into my ear, "As long as I'm with you, whatever we do will be cool. We can always do the movie next weekend."

I beamed a little. I was so lucky—I had a boyfriend who cared about me.

"I don't know what I should wear!" I lamented to Courtney as we lay in the Room, scanning celebrity magazines.

"Wear to what?" Taylor plopped down beside me.

"Um." If I didn't tell Taylor about the party, she was sure to find out about it afterward and be mad at me. But if I invited her, it would be really awkward, wouldn't it? The Trinity weren't big fans of hers, and vice versa. And the Trinity were my best friends, not Taylor.

"I'm having this thing at my house, um, hotel, on Friday, if you want to come." I had to mention it. I would feel guilty if I didn't. After all, her parents hadn't only split up—her father had come out of the closet as well! I gave a glance to Courtney to see how she would react. She stayed silent, staring intently at the fashion don'ts of the past week.

Taylor nodded. "Okay, sure. Where is it?"

"The Four Seasons. At eight o'clockish. You can sleep over if you want."

Now I felt better about the situation. I was being charitable and nice to Taylor, who didn't have that many friends except for those weird drama kids.

"See you then."

It was Friday, and Alissa, Kim, Courtney, and I were tearing apart my closet and their suitcases full of designer couture, searching for something appropriate to wear.

"Here, wear this!" Kim suggested, pushing a short, sequined black dress toward me. "My mom brought it home from some Oscar party gift bag last year."

I nodded. Every time one of the Trinity brought up her

mother, I was reminded of the conversation I had over-heard at the beginning of the year. It had to be one of them who had joined MUN because her mother had told her to. And who had gotten a boob job. I hadn't ever spent much time with the Trinity before this year—and hadn't been examining their breast sizes—so I really had no idea who it was.

I pulled the dress on. It hugged my curves tightly; self-consciously, I walked to the mirror. From behind me, Alissa said, "Wow, Becky. You look totally hot."

I examined myself. I wondered if I even dared to have the thought—but, I did look good. I, brainy Becky Miller, looked hot. And, even better, the coolest girl in the grade was acknowledging it.

After we were all dressed, we teetered to the elevator and down to the lobby. Aaron arrived soon after, and we threw multicolored streamers over one area of the cock-tail lounge adjacent to the hotel lobby. I had called the woman at the concierge's desk and arranged the logistics of the evening. It would be very small, I promised, and we wouldn't cause a disturbance. The woman was a big fan of my mother and, after asking me what it was like to live with such a style guru, she said yes.

There weren't that many of us that night. My mom suggested that I invite Joey, but I had said no. He was a good person to have an intellectual conversation with, but I wasn't sure that he and my new friends would mesh well. I often found that I had to stop myself from injecting political anecdotes or literary references into my conversations with them. It wasn't "cool" to discuss academic issues outside of classes, I had learned. Besides, I hadn't been talking with Joey very much recently. Between the Trinity, Aaron, June, and my parents, I was pretty much talked out.

I wasn't that close with Taylor anymore either, but nonetheless, she came to the Four Seasons that night, trailed by her father. She wore an elegant long purple dress with a satin bodice and a petticoat underneath, which made the skirt very voluminous. I felt uncomfortable for her. Her dress would have fit better in the eighteenth century than at a cocktail lounge. When she entered the room, Alissa nudged me. "You invited her?" she said.

I shrugged. "Yeah. I guess I felt sort of bad for her."

"That was nice of you," Alissa said, but I could tell she didn't really mean it. "She doesn't really have any friends."

I knew that wasn't true, that what Alissa meant was that Taylor's friends weren't worth talking to . . . or about.

Taylor came to sit down on a couch next to Aaron and me. Aaron put his hand forward to introduce himself to Taylor and then, smiling, said, "Interesting dress. Is it Renaissance reenactment month?"

I chuckled, but stopped myself when I saw Taylor's face.

"Thanks!" Taylor said. "My father designed it. He's got better fashion sense than most guys." She was smiling, and Aaron didn't immediately catch the veiled insult in her words. But Aaron hadn't meant his comment as an insult—he was just making a joke. Why did Taylor have to take things so personally?

Taylor's dad, clad in electric orange jeans and a retro blazer, explained that he wanted to get pictures of Taylor, out and about and wearing his new creation, and then he'd "skedaddle" (his exact word). Taylor posed dramatically for a few shots, and then her dad passed the camera to me and asked if I would take a picture of the two of them. I stood up from the couch so that I could capture the entire dress. "Gorgeous. Thank you, doll," her dad said, and then he said good-bye to Taylor and left.

"Doll?" Aaron snickered into my ear. I shushed him. I understood why he was upset, though. Taylor had made fun of him, bruised his ego. And, as I was discovering, although Aaron's ego was large, it was also very fragile. I thought that was endearing.

Not long after Mr. Tremaine had gone, Courtney's stepmother, Marisa, showed up to drop off Courtney's sleepover bag, which Courtney had forgotten at home. This parent-free evening sure involved a lot of parents.

"Becky, hello, darling," Marisa said, leaning in to give me a kiss on each cheek. "I loved meeting your mother and her friends at that meeting the other day. They're all so *fascinating*."

Courtney shot me a look. Her pale, freckled cheeks had begun to turn pink.

Marisa deposited Courtney's duffel bag on a couch and then reached into her oversized pink purse. She pulled out a bottle of Absolut Raspberry vodka and placed it in my hands. "I didn't know if you guys had anything yummy, so I brought a treat," she said, winking at me. "Okay, Courtney, I'm going to head out now. Have fun with your friends tonight!" She turned around and walked across the lobby, her heels clicking with each step.

In order to avoid the awkwardness of the situation, I got drunk. I wasn't the only one to drink—everyone, except for Taylor, took turns taking swigs from the bottle of Absolut and traveling over to the bar to "order" martinis. I found that all it took was a wink and a little cleavage, and the bartender wouldn't card.

I woke up the next morning feeling fuzzy. I was in my twin bed wearing pajama pants but no shirt. Aaron was pressed against my back. I stood up, suddenly wide awake, despite a headache shooting through my skull. Courtney was passed out on the twin bed next to mine, which meant that Alissa and Kim were probably on the pullout bed next door. Jack had stayed at Dad's. Who knows where Taylor was. Conscious of my seminakedness, I covered my chest with one hand and reached down to grope along the floor with the other, looking for my shirt.

What had happened?

Let's Talk About Sex

*T*he next day, when I arrived at my dad's house, I found Jack, Dad, and Darcy sprawled on my dad's king-sized bed, watching *South Park*. I hated seeing Darcy in that bed. My mother used to sleep in that bed. And when I was really little, I would sneak into their room in the middle of the night and crawl into that bed, right between my mom and my dad. Now this twentysomething tart slept there instead.

"Hi, sweetheart, how are you? Oh—someone named Aaron called looking for you. He said you weren't picking up your cell phone?" my dad said. It wasn't that I was ignoring his calls. I still hadn't been able to remember what had happened on Friday night, and I wasn't sure that

I even wanted to know.

Jack sat up. "Who's Aaron, Becky?" His voice was sing-songy. He knew damn well who Aaron was; he just wanted to make me say it in front of Dad. And Darcy.

"Aaron's my boyfriend." I looked my dad straight in the eye. I spoke quickly, before I could second-guess myself. Suddenly, I found myself feeling as though I were in some twisted position of power. I smirked at Darcy, who was lying down, wrapped around my dad. My dad could have a girlfriend. Well, I could have a boyfriend, too. And I could do inappropriate things with him if I wanted to (what things, I wished I knew). I was basically an adult, after all.

"Well," Dad said, putting his arm around Darcy, "if he approves of you, I approve of him."

"That . . ." I began. I stopped myself. Pardon? *If he approves of you, I approve of him?* That certainly wasn't how that line was supposed to go. It was backward, and delib-erately so. I nodded my head. Still trying to wrap my head around the sentence, I left the room, not feeling my best. I had always imagined that when I finally told my dad that I had a boyfriend, it would be a triumphant moment. And this? This didn't feel so triumphant.

I managed to make it through the weekend without checking Facebook. I wanted to ignore the goings-on of Friday night for as long as I possibly could. So, I immersed myself—as I had many times before—in MUN work. The MUN conference was just a week away, and we were busy preparing and solidifying our speeches and arguments.

Courtney finally understood who Uganda's allies were, which was crucial for resolution writing. And I was feeling a little more comfortable about having her as my delegation partner.

Mr. Elwright was concerned about some of the girls in class being more enthusiastic about the boys at the upcoming weekend conference than about the conference itself. He was especially concerned about what those girls might wear. He had cocked his chin toward Alissa, whose skirt was rolled over so many times that it was significantly shorter than the striped boxer shorts she was wearing, and then had asked me to explain Western business attire to the girls, before blushing and leaving the room to "run a quick errand" (read: so he could be as far from this conversation as possible).

"So," I told a group of tired-looking girls, "this weekend, at the conference, there is a dress code, as most of you know." I tried to think of a way to tell everyone to look their best without looking slutty. "They call it 'Western business attire,' which basically means that even if you are representing Saudi Arabia, you can't wear an abaya." I paused. Blank faces stared back at me. "An abaya is what women wear in Saudi Arabia to cover themselves head to toe," I explained. More blank looks. "Anyway, as far as clothes for MUN go, whatever you wear, make sure you look professional. We want to be paid attention to because of our brains, not our bodies. So don't wear jeans, and no skintight skirts or low-cut shirts."

Most of the girls laughed or snickered, but Alissa winked at me. Why was she winking?

"Have you and Aaron had sex?" Katie Roberts, a bubbly sophomore, asked me after the meeting ended.

"What?"

Courtney's eyes were on me now.

"You know . . . should we add you to the list?" When I didn't respond, Katie added, "You know, there's that picture up of you with a condom in your mouth, so some people have been assuming . . ."

What?

A condom? In my mouth? Did that mean . . . ? Fuck. What the hell had I been thinking, getting so drunk?

"No." I shook my head, my heart racing. "No. I shouldn't be on the list," I said. I hadn't had sex. I would have remembered that, or at least part of that, right?

That night, I browsed through the pictures that Alissa had added to Facebook from the past Friday's festivities. I searched for a photo featuring me and a condom, and before long, I found it. I squinted my eyes at the computer screen, looking at a girl I could barely identify as myself.

There I was, my eyes dilated, sitting on Aaron's lap. Indeed, there was not one but two condoms in my mouth—both of them in their wrappers. And next to me, on the other side of Aaron, was my little brother.

My little brother? What was he doing there? I

concentrated for a minute and tried to dedicate my brain power to remembering what had happened that night. Bits and pieces were coming back to me.

Jack had entered the lounge holding a cell phone in one hand and pulling up his pants with the other. "Mom says I can do whatever you guys are doing before she takes me to Dad's," Jack said. "So pass me the booze."

"Hey," Aaron said, eyeing my brother, his eyebrows furrowed together. "I know you. I mean, I've met you before. I don't know where, though."

Jack rolled his eyes. "I'm in your computer science class." Aaron's face was blank. "I sit one row behind you, idiot," Jack added.

"Oh!" Aaron nodded his head eagerly. "That's right!" His hands were wrapped around my waist, and he pulled me back to kiss him.

"My brother!" I hissed, pulling away. Kissing in public was one thing, but kissing in front of my little brother? Well, that was something else entirely.

Jack smirked and pulled up a chair. He sat down and dug a hand into his jeans pocket. "Here," he said, holding up a couple of condoms. "You might want these."

"Why do you have condoms?" I asked Jack, sitting back upright and smoothing out my hair.

"Why wouldn't I?" He took a swig from the vodka bottle. "No glove, no love." Jack tossed the condoms to me.

Suddenly I was starving and a little queasy. I had been

drinking on an empty stomach. "Unless this is edible, I don't want it," I said.

Alissa took out her camera. Or maybe she'd had it out the whole time. I was too drunk to tell. "Put it in your mouth. Pretend it's food," she said, cracking up as if she'd just told a really, really good joke.

"That is so funny. Yeah, Becky, do it!" Kim added.

So I did.

It wasn't that I was nervous about sex itself; I was just nervous about being naked in front of someone else. Because after you had sex, when you were just going about your normal, clothed life, there that other person would be. And he would have seen you without your clothes on; he would know what you looked like underneath that dress.

And there was something intrinsically terrifying about that.

So when I had woken up minus my shirt and next to Aaron, I had been nervous.

Although my memories of that evening took a few days to resurface, eventually they did. I was pleased to discover that I hadn't had sex with Aaron. I had come pretty close, though. Aaron and I had been sitting side by side on one of the twin beds in my room, our backs up against the headboard, surfing channels on the television. Alissa had decided suddenly that she had to have an ice cream sundae, and Courtney and Kim had accompanied her downstairs to instruct the kitchen—under no circumstances were there to be any nuts on top of the whipped cream.

"My feet hurt," Aaron had said, wriggling the toes within his white socks.

"Mine, too," I'd said, emphasizing the patent leather heels that I hadn't removed when we had sat down on the bed, simply because I thought they made my legs look longer, and Aaron hadn't noticed them yet.

Aaron had looked down toward my feet, nodded, and looked back up at the TV. A few minutes later, he had clicked the OFF button on the TV remote and turned his head toward me.

"You're beautiful," he had slurred. Even though he was drunk, the compliment meant a lot to me. Aaron's lips had met mine as he'd leaned in toward me, pushing his hand down on the bed for leverage. His eyes were closed even before our lips had made contact. Once we were touching, I'd closed mine but then proceeded to open them again, just to make sure that Aaron's were still closed. He'd put his arms around me and kissed me, his hand wandering to the small of my back. My insides had felt fluttery and my sense of control had faded—in a good way, for once. But that, too, might have been because of the alcohol. Aaron had reached up my back to unzip the dress. I knew where his hand was headed, but when it had touched my back, a shiver had shot down my spine and my arms had fallen to my sides.

"Okay?" Aaron had asked.

"Yeah." I'd nodded, looking up at him. His hair was

rumpled and his cheeks were flushed. It was moments like these when I couldn't believe I was actually going out with him. I'd felt weightless and giddy. He was unzipping my dress, pulling it all the way down past my waist. I was nervous, afraid that Aaron wouldn't like what he saw. That extra fat right below my belly button, my none-too-large breasts, everything. But Aaron, kissing my neck and then downward, had just taken a breath, looked up at me, and said, "Beautiful." I had relaxed into him, enjoying his touch and my light-headedness. We'd fooled around until we were both too tired to kiss. I'd fallen asleep in his arms.

We both slept in that twin bed, and I had felt entirely at peace. The warmth of Aaron's body behind mine protected me. I was desired. I was happy.

Facebook Wars

*T*aylor had posted some pictures from my party, too. Aaron told me about them over the phone.

I balanced the phone on my ear and leaned forward to type Taylor's name into the search box. Sure enough, she had a new album up, entitled "Tipsy." Most of the pictures were ones that Taylor's father had taken, before we were all drunk, while we still had the capability to smile like normal people. The best picture was of Taylor and her dad. Taylor's dress looked pretty (albeit out of place), and the color saturation on her dad's salmon-colored pants was intense. They were both smiling. I scrolled down the page to leave a comment on the photo: *Adorable.*

"This picture of Taylor and her dad is pretty cute," I

told Aaron, still balancing the phone on my shoulder.

"You mean the one where he looks gay?"

I gulped and grabbed onto the phone. "Don't say that," I said.

"Why not? It's funny."

"Not really," I said.

"Whatever, Miss Serious."

"I have to go."

Aaron didn't know, I reasoned. He was a guy—a lot of guys called things "gay," no matter how inappropriate it might be. He had no idea. He didn't know that Taylor's dad actually was gay. I threw the phone across my bed and pressed the COMMENT button on Facebook. I was just glad that Aaron had made the "gay" comment to me, not to Taylor.

The next day at school, I was careful to be extra nice to Taylor. I thought being nice might make up for the fact that, unbeknownst to her, Aaron had been such a jerk.

But then it all went to shit. After school, I received an e-mail from Taylor. The e-mail had no subject and had only one line in it. *Your boyfriend is a jackass*, it read. I switched into my instant messenger application and searched for Taylor's screen name in my buddy list. She was online, so I sent her a message. I asked why she thought my boyfriend was a jackass, and did she understand that I didn't really appreciate her calling him a jackass?

Check Facebook, she told me. *Then you'll understand. And thanks for blabbing.*

What? I went to her page and saw that Aaron had left a comment on the photo of Taylor and her father.

It read: *Your dad looks so gay in this picture.*

"Shit," I said to my empty room.

I didn't say anything, I wrote to Taylor. *He doesn't know. If he knew, he'd never have said that.*

Maybe, Taylor wrote back.

Can I tell him? I asked.

NO.

Why? I messaged back. Taylor had said that it wasn't a secret; so why couldn't I tell Aaron?

Because I said so. Because he wouldn't get it.

I should have said something to Aaron. I should have done something to stop it. I should have, I would have, I could have. But I didn't. Instead, I just ignored Aaron and his calls while the online drama exploded.

Everything happened over the Internet—no phone calls, no face-to-face meetings, just uncensored, online viciousness. That's the problem with the Internet. Online, people have the courage to say things they would never dare say to someone's face. Typing sort of takes away responsibility for the situation; you are detached from what you're writing—the computer screen acts as a buffer.

June would say that this is why I like to write so much—because when I write something down, I automatically become one step removed from the incident. But this is different. I just keep a journal and write papers from the viewpoints of different countries.

I don't go around harassing my girlfriend's friend online.

The problem was that Aaron didn't know about Taylor's dad. He was obnoxious, sure, but everything he said was made worse by the fact that Taylor's dad actually *was* gay.

Over the next few days, Taylor and Aaron had an increasingly heated online conversation, all of which was published on Facebook for hundreds of people to see. Because I was the first person to comment on the photo, I received an e-mail notification any time someone else commented on it. And because my e-mail came to my phone, which I never turned off—even during the school day, when cell phones were strictly off-limits—I was constantly in the loop. Although, more than once, I wished that I wasn't. Taylor's first message was a very calm response to Aaron, chastising him for believing that political incorrectness was "cool."

Then the trouble started. My phone buzzed in math class the next day. Aaron had responded to Taylor's message. *I didn't mean to imply that he looked gay—as in bad—but rather that he looked gay—as in homosexual. Therefore, it is entirely politically correct,* he wrote. I winced as I read through the post. *We all know he isn't gay, so quit making a big deal about it.*

Wrong. So wrong.

It just got worse and worse until it finally hit a low, and this message popped up:

Say sorry, you self-righteous do-gooder freak. What the hell is your problem? Obviously, you're wrong. Oh—and it's pissing me off that you're singling me out (and Becky, too, I assume) simply for a comment. I don't like you, and I don't think she does either. Give me a break. Seriously, what is your problem? I say that a stupid picture looks gay and you go crazy? Get a life. And quit harassing me.

By the weekend, the first day of the MUN Conference, Taylor and I had stopped speaking. I knew that, if I wanted to be a good friend, I should have commented on the photo on Facebook to say that Aaron was a jerk. But I didn't—I couldn't.

Every time I saw Taylor begin to walk toward me in the hallway, I would swing my tote bag over my shoulder, turn around, and walk in the opposite direction. I could have just told her that what Aaron said wasn't true—that I did like her—but I was too scared that Aaron might get mad at me, and that I might be forced to choose between the Trinity and Taylor.

Diplomacy

*T*hat weekend, when the Whitbread MUN team met up at UC Berkeley to walk to opening ceremonies, I ignored Taylor, and she ignored me.

"So," I told Alissa and Courtney, "my friend Joey Michaels is going to be here today. He's really nice. You'll like him, I think. Courtney, he's in our committee."

Mr. Elwright, juggling a pile of binders and name tags, shot me a look and cocked his head to Kim.

"Kim, *what* are you wearing?" I asked while passing out agendas to the team.

Kim smiled. "Western business attire! Isn't this outfit so cute? I love pretending to be a businessperson!" Kim was wearing a skintight leopard-print skirt matched with a cut-down-to-there V-neck sweater. And unlike me, she had boobs to show off.

I, too, had spent extra time getting ready that morning. Underneath my white button-down and tank top, I had on a lacy orange push-up bra and, underneath my pinstripe pants, a matching thong. I wondered how Aaron would react when he saw them.

"Okay," I told the group, "we'll meet back in the dining hall for dinner, after our committee sessions. Good luck. I know you'll be great."

My committee was meeting in a large lecture hall. The session hadn't started yet, so kids in business wear chatted with each other; some even tried to jump the gun and begin making allies. I scanned the room and found Joey and Aaron sitting toward the middle. I made my way over to say hello.

"You ready for this?" I said, smiling playfully. The Stratfield boys were representing South Africa, so I anticipated that they could be counted on to ally with us, Uganda.

"You're going down," Aaron said, smiling.

I smiled back, trying to hide a slight uneasiness at his tough words.

"There are approximately 1.7 million AIDS orphans in Uganda, and over 11 million AIDS orphans in all of sub-Saharan Africa. This is not just Uganda's issue. This is a global issue. We need to increase HIV/AIDS awareness and education in order to prevent the increased transmission of the disease as well as to decrease the stigma surrounding AIDS orphans in Uganda, and in Africa as a whole. Please join us and sign Resolution A–1."

Amid applause, I made my way back to my seat in the third row. "That was great!" Courtney said. "You didn't look nervous at all. And you made eye contact with people. Mr. Elwright said that's important."

Iceland, a dark-haired boy with a popped collar, poked my back. "Notes for you," he said. In Model United Nations, note passing is an official form of communication. Countries can form allies and work on resolutions through notes (as well as gossip and flirt). I had sent a note to South Africa saying, *J and A—want to be a sponsor of our resolution?* ♥ *Uganda.*

Now, I received their reply. In Aaron's handwriting was *Nope. We're doing our own resolution. May the best team win.* My stomach dropped. Why were they doing this? South Africa, as a country, supported our stance on AIDS education. It would be better for both of us to write one resolution, not two, because that way, other countries wouldn't have to choose between two very similar resolutions. I twisted my head to Joey and Aaron and held my hands up, eyebrows wrinkled. Joey shrugged his shoulders and pointed to Aaron. I scowled. Sure, this was a competition, and not every team could win, but the core of this conference was supposed to be *diplomacy.*

South Africa was a few countries after Uganda on the speakers list, so, a few minutes later, Joey and Aaron walked up to the podium to speak. Joey began by introducing South Africa's stance on the issue of AIDS awareness.

Courtney elbowed me. "Is that Joey?" I nodded. She crinkled her eyebrows, examining him. "I mean, I guess he's okay-looking, but his Western business attire is so awkward. Plus, he looks like he's totally nervous." I just shrugged.

After a minute or two, Joey stepped back, and Aaron took the microphone. "Everyone here should sign onto Resolution A–2, not A–1. Our resolution is going to be *so* much better than theirs. Besides, who would you rather have on your side, Uganda or South Africa? Uganda's all talk and no action." Aaron flashed a winning smile. I felt my insides churning. Why was he doing this? Was he being deliberately mean to me? Joey shot me a sympathetic look as he walked back to his seat, but I looked away.

Once their speech was over, I shot my hand and my placard into the air, hoping to be called on as one of the country responses. After each speech, two countries were allowed to make comments. I waved my placard wildly in the air. I must have looked desperate. Courtney tugged at my sleeve. "Relax," she told me. But I couldn't. I was called on to be the second comment, and, shaking, I made my way to the front of the room.

I wanted to win this, I really did. But I didn't want to have to play dirty. "I would like to invite you all, including South Africa, to join in signing Resolution A–1. I believe that a merger of the two resolutions would best serve the interests of the United Nations and create a more force-ful resolution." And that was when I knocked down the podium. I widened my eyes in shock as the podium, micro-phone and all, toppled onto the ground. A high-pitched squeak reverberated through the room, causing people to clamp their hands over their ears. I just wanted to disap-pear. One of the committee chairs was shaking her head. There was no way I was going to win this now.

After dinner that night, the Whitbread and Stratfield teams mingled in the dining hall, discussing the day's events. I stood with Kim and Alissa, who were regaling me with tales of the notes they had received. Taylor was talking with Joey, and Courtney was chatting with Aaron.

"Is that Joey?" Alissa asked, gesturing her head toward him. "You know, the one who's talking with *her*?"

I nodded.

"Oh. He looks like kind of a geek. No offense."

I nodded again. I didn't understand. Why did peo-ple—Aaron in particular—have to be such jerks? I caught Taylor's eye. She shot me a cold, almost nasty look. *Shit,* I thought. *I really screwed things up with her.*

Later, Aaron snuck into my hotel room while Court-ney was in Kim and Alissa's room. "Hey," he said, closing the door quietly behind him. He was still wearing his button-down and khakis, but the shirt was wrinkled and unbuttoned at the top. He looked hot. This was the moment I had been waiting for, the moment when I would show off my new lingerie. But it wasn't right. I crossed my arms over my chest, self-consciously. He climbed onto the bed and pressed his mouth against mine, but I gathered up my willpower and pushed him away.

"Why did you do that today, in committee? You humiliated me—my country—for no reason! We're allies, Aaron. In the real world, at least. And what's more, you're my boyfriend! You're supposed to be nice to me, not mean." My voice was rising.

"Geez. Overreact much?" He seemed to think this was a joke because he then grabbed hold of my mouth once more. Once more, I pulled away. I had started standing up for myself, and I wasn't going to stop.

"And what you said to Taylor was wrong. You told her I agreed with you, but I don't."

"Oh, so Miss Public Speaker didn't even have the guts to tell Taylor herself, huh? I guess that just goes to show how brave you are. Or maybe it's because you only like doing the *popular* thing?"

I shoved him away. This was getting nasty.

"Leave," I said. "Just leave."

"You guys are the perfect couple," Courtney told me later, while we brushed our teeth in the bathroom. "It's just a rough patch."

I shrugged. I wasn't so sure about that. Aaron had sent me a text message after he left, telling me that we needed to talk. I knew that could be code for only one thing.

Part of me wanted to break up with him, but most of me didn't. I was afraid that I wouldn't be able to find another boyfriend, and I was afraid that the Trinity wouldn't like me as much without him.

I was getting into bed when the phone rang. "Hey," Aaron said, his voice warm.

"Hey," I replied, and suddenly it seemed like, maybe, everything would be okay.

"Tell me why I shouldn't break up with you. Why should I stay in a relationship with you? Tell me how important I am to you."

"What?" Not what I was expecting. He wanted me to beg him to stay with me, to plead my case as to why I should remain his girlfriend?

"I, um, I have to go. I'll call you back." I hung up the phone quickly. His question had startled me. What was I doing, allowing myself to be treated like this? Was it all for the sake of popularity? All so that I could call three coke-snorting, binge-drinking girls my friends? This couldn't possibly be worth it.

"What's going on?" Courtney asked me, as I shoved my feet into my flats and headed for the door.

"Nothing," I said, fighting back tears. I didn't want to have this conversation in front of her. I didn't want to seem weak.

Closing the door behind me, I dialed Aaron's number. "I'm not going to list the reasons why you should stay with me, or go on and on about how important you are to me. Because you know what? I don't need you, Aaron Winters. And if you can't make the decision whether or not to break up with me, then I will. We're over," I said, all in one breath. I realized that my hands were shaking as I waited for Aaron's response.

"Okay. Um, so, I guess that's it."

"Yeah." There was an awkward silence, and then, I added, "I have to go." I hung up the phone.

"What happened?" Courtney asked when I reentered the room.

"Aaron and I just broke up." I leaned against the door. Saying it out loud made it real, and it hurt.

Eyes wide, she said, "So, are you going to change your Facebook relationship status?"

I almost laughed. I figured that would be better than crying. Instead I just nodded, reached for my laptop, and clicked the button to edit my profile. Within one minute, I went from IN A RELATIONSHIP to SINGLE. And every one of the couple hundred people I was "friends" with on Facebook would soon know it.

Breaking Up Is Hard to Do

A few minutes after I broke up with Aaron on the phone, there was a knock at my hotel room door. Warily, I opened it. Joey stood before me wearing his button-down shirt and boxers.

"Sorry," he said, catching me looking at his bare legs. "I forgot to put on pants, but I wanted to tell you right away, before you heard from someone else or . . ." He trailed off, the adrenaline draining from his voice.

"What?" I said, scanning his face. "What's going on?"

"It's Aaron," he said, his voice now quiet. I realized that he might have been in the room for Aaron's half of the breakup conversation. That made me feel embarrassed, and worse, vulnerable. At the mention of Aaron's name, my heart rate picked up. "He just posted this note on Facebook. About you and your relationship with him. I tried to convince him not to do it, it's just disrespectful and obnoxious and totally immature!" Joey stamped his bare foot against the carpeted floor, indignant. He nodded toward Courtney's laptop, which lay open on my bed. "You should probably see it for yourself."

I didn't know what the note said, but I could guess that it wasn't full of nice memories and compliments. "Thanks," I said to Joey, "for standing up to Aaron. You didn't have to. I mean, I wouldn't want you to deal with shit as a result of this."

Joey shrugged. "So maybe I'll be less popular at school for a week or so. What does that matter, really? When it comes down to it, you just have to do what you think is right."

I wondered how it was possible that Joey could really not care about popularity. I hated having to buy into the vanity and superficiality of the social ladder, but I did it anyway. And why did I do it, again?

I logged onto Facebook and began to look for the note. Here's the great thing about Facebook: It's very easy to stay up-to-date with what your Facebook "friends" are doing. Here's the not-so-great thing about Facebook: It's very easy to stay up-to-date with what your Facebook "friends" are doing. Right on Aaron's profile page, the same page that would appear for every one of Aaron's six hundred friends, was the first paragraph of his note. My adrenaline pumping, I clicked on it.

Aaron had written two full pages detailing our relationship and our breakup. At the beginning, he pronounced that our relationship had been mostly physical—that there really wasn't that much emotion in it. He didn't love me, he said; he wasn't even that attracted to me. At the bottom, he had included a photo of the two of us. I was smiling at the camera, and he was smiling at me, his arms wrapped around my waist.

His words stung me. I had trusted him. I had trusted that he wouldn't hurt me. And now, here he was telling several hundred people—many of them people I knew—that he hadn't really liked me that much after all. I felt cheap, and I felt used. Drawing back from the computer screen, I remembered that Courtney and Joey were still in the room. I wasn't going to cry. Not in front of them, at least. Joey and Courtney were standing together, talking. "That was a good speech you made today," Joey said to Courtney.

"Thanks," Courtney said, looking away, searching for a way out of the conversation.

Joey could tell that Courtney wasn't interested in talking with him, and he shifted uncomfortably. "I'm sorry, Becky," he said to me.

"No, it's fine," I said. "I'm fine."

But I wasn't. I wasn't fine at all.

The rest of the conference was a blur. I didn't get much sleep. I was on autopilot, deflecting attacks from Aaron (he'd passed a note that read, *Blonde Uganda is a bitch. Don't sponsor her resolution. Resist!*), trying to ignore the fact that the Trinity were more concerned with my popularity status than my dignity (Alissa had told me to not stand up to Aaron because he was a popular guy and it wouldn't be good to make him my enemy), and trying to kick some MUN ass.

In my final speech, I stressed the importance of diplomacy. I wish I could've delivered the speech directly to Aaron, but he turned away every time I looked in his general direction.

"Fellow delegates," I said in conclusion, "we are brought here today as diplomats. We must represent the ideals of our countries, but more important than that, we must work together. A diplomat is tactful and handles situations so that there is little or no ill will. If we don't all work together, then nothing can be accomplished. In the international community, the voice of one holds little strength compared to the voices of many. Let us join together as the voices of many. Let us be the voices that make a difference. Thank you."

There was silence for a moment, and then applause erupted. My face flushed, I stepped down from the podium.

Sitting in a large auditorium at the closing ceremonies, I was nervous. Nervous, first and foremost, that Aaron would win. He sat two rows in front of me, and, as the winners from each committee were announced, I watched the back of his head. Finally, the secretary general of the conference took the podium to announce the winner of the gavel—the highest award. The gavel went to only one delegate.

The secretary general announced: "Becky Miller."

I shook with adrenaline as I edged my way out of the row I was sitting in and walked up the aisle. As I passed Aaron's row, I shot him a triumphant look.

But that triumph didn't last long.

Friends Like These (Part Two)

*S*unday night I was back at the Four Seasons when I received an instant message from Courtney. *I just thought I should let you know,* she began, *that I'm going out with Aaron.*

What the hell? I wrote.

I've liked him for a while now, and, well, this weekend, things just sort of fell into place.

Fell into place? Meaning that I broke up with Aaron, so now she could go out with him?

Okay? Courtney added.

Furious, I dug through my backpack for my journal. Pausing to uncap a pen, I began a new Shit List.

Not okay. I was not okay. This was not okay. Friends

were supposed to come before boys. And this wasn't just any boy, this was the boy that I broke up with yesterday and who had since proceeded to launch an attack against me. I started the list by writing *Best friend (former?) going out with ex-boyfriend*. It hurt even more that Aaron—who was my first . . . everything—had presumably also given Courtney her first kiss.

Fabulous. I couldn't wait for school on Monday.

I wanted it to die down, to go away. I wanted Aaron to apologize for trying to sabotage me at the conference, and I wanted Courtney to break up with Aaron. I wanted Aaron to admit that he was only going out with Courtney because he thought it would get to me, and that he didn't really like her.

On Monday, seeing as I hadn't slept all night anyway, I started getting ready for school half an hour early. Sure, I had been through a thunderstorm and everyone knew about it, but that was all the more reason to take extra steps to look fabulous. Besides, Aaron had moved on to Courtney, and with her long red waves and acne-free face, I had a lot to live up to.

After biology, I made my way to the Room, where I found Alissa, Kim, and Courtney huddled around a laptop. I weaved my way through the room, over to them. As I walked, everyone was silent. Or maybe I was just imagining that. "How's it going?" I said to Alissa and Kim. I faced away from Courtney.

Alissa closed the laptop. "We're fine," she said. "And you?"

"I'm good. Everything's fine." Could she see me sweating? Was it in my mind, or did Alissa seem more hostile than usual? There was silence as we stood staring at each other. Finally, I said, "Well, I guess I should go to class. See you later?"

"Bye."

I didn't actually have class—it was my free period. But I couldn't stay in the Room. As I walked out, I caught Taylor's eye. She had been sitting on the opposite side of the room, toward the door. Had she seen the whole thing? She quickly looked away.

That day, I spent my break, lunch, and free periods in the library, reading a plastic-covered copy of *The Bell Jar*. Sylvia Plath was the marker that let me know I was sinking into depression. When I was depressed, I liked to read about others who were more depressed than me. It made me feel less alone, but it also didn't help my emotional well-being. In the seventh grade, we had to create a poetry anthology on a subject of our choice. I chose depression. I included Sylvia Plath poems, mostly, but I also wrote a few of my own. One was about paralyzing anxiety, another about feeling suffocated by darkness. I maintained the position that my poetry was fictional; I was trying to take on the persona of someone—not me—who was depressed.

Now, I felt both darkness and anxiety taking hold of

me. I hadn't changed my pharmaceutical cocktail, but in my mind things were growing bleaker.

Taylor was the only other person in English class when I arrived later that day. I set my books down on the table and walked over to her. "I'm really sorry about what happened on Facebook," I said. "I should have said something, I know. I knew Aaron was wrong, but I guess I was just so excited about having a boyfriend, and I was afraid of screwing it up."

"So you wait until now—now, when you've got nothing else to lose—to say something. That's very sweet of you." Her voice dripped with sarcasm. "Don't think I didn't see it. I knew I was second banana to those whores. And I knew you didn't like them to see you hanging out with me because you were afraid it would reflect badly on you. So don't think that now, when you've got no friends left, you can come crawling back to me and I'll accept you."

After school, desperate for a friend, I called Amanda. We hadn't talked on the phone since Halloween. She didn't even know much about Aaron. We had instant messaged back and forth, but usually, Amanda was so busy telling me about all the parties and openings she was attending that she forgot to ask about my life and how I was doing. This afternoon, I told her about the breakup situation. Her advice to me? "Just drop it. If you want to stay friends with them, you have to suck it up. You shouldn't be mad about

Courtney going out with him; you should consider your-self lucky that you managed to land them as friends and that someone as pretty and popular as Courtney would go out with your ex-boyfriend."

"What?" I said. "Are you joking?"

She wasn't. And then she got off the phone as quickly as possible with an excuse about her dad needing her to run lines with him in the other room.

Now, when I was explaining the weekend to my mom, I added Amanda to the list of people who were currently making my life difficult.

"That's awful about Amanda," Mom said when I finally broke down and told her about what had been happening. "But that Taylor situation—that's really tough. You apolo-gized, which is all you can do. Now you'll just have to see if, with time and effort, you can build back that relation-ship. Taylor seems like a sweet girl, and God knows you could use more of those in your life right now."

Pam Michaels was on her way up, so I excused myself to my room. I didn't want to see anyone right then. I opened up one of the bags I had packed at my dad's house—it was always an elaborate production each week, packing up and hoping that I remembered everything I needed, like Prozac, for instance—but I couldn't find my biology textbook. I looked through my backpack and then in the drawers of my desk, but the book wasn't there. I had a test the next day. I didn't usually do the nightly worksheets for bio, but I found that if I just read over the chapter the night before the test, I could get an A. It was pretty easy to remember what I'd read; I could even visualize the pages and what information had been on which particular page. But if I didn't have the textbook, I would have no way of knowing what I had to know.

I could have left the book at school, but I didn't think I had brought it that day. I called my dad to see if I had left it at his house. I didn't usually forget or misplace things; I was always good about keeping track of my possessions. In fact, sometimes I was even *too* good at it. But ever since this whole Aaron fiasco had erupted, I felt less and less on top of the goings-on in my life.

Finally, Dad picked up. I asked about the textbook. "Becky," Dad sighed, sounding as if I had caught him at a bad time. The trouble was, with my dad, it was always a bad time. "I don't even know what your books look like!"

"Of course you don't!" I stood up, suddenly enraged. "You don't know anything about my life! God forbid you might actually act like my *father* and pay attention once in a while!" I hung up and fell face first onto my bed, trying to stifle my tears.

My mom and Pam were in the other room, probably talking about ways to make this hotel room more of a home. I had to get out of this place.

I gathered my wallet, keys, and cell phone, dumped them in a purse, and hurried through the room. Mom called my name. I just told her I'd be back and kept walking, out the door, down the hall, and into the fresh air.

The valet brought me my car, but I had no idea where to go. I couldn't go to my dad's—not after I had yelled at him. I didn't want to deal with that. I couldn't call the Trinity, I couldn't call Amanda, and I couldn't call Taylor. So I just got in the car and drove, and before long, I found myself cruising through the streets of Hancock Park. I drove past my dad's house and past Amanda's old house. I drove down Larchmont, but I didn't get out for a coffee because I was afraid that I would run into someone I knew, and I was afraid that I might burst into tears at any moment.

As I drove past Whitbread, I dialed June Kauffman's emergency number, half expecting to get her answering service. But she picked up immediately. I was so relieved to have her on the phone that I let out a long sigh. It felt like I'd been holding my breath forever. After I confessed to her that I hadn't slept in the past three days, she scheduled me for an extra appointment, on Friday.

A few minutes later, Joey called me. "Hey," he said. "My mom called me and said something about you rushing out of your mom's place and not telling anyone where you were going. Are you okay?"

I felt tears welling up in my eyes.

I shook my head, even though I knew Joey couldn't see it. "No," I said finally. As June had warned me, if I didn't own up to my emotions, I might be forever trapped inside myself. And I didn't want that. I started to cry, my breath coming in short bursts, my nose sniffling.

"Where are you?"

"I'm in Hancock Park."

"Come to my house."

Joey was sitting on the chair swing in his front yard when I arrived. Self-conscious, I got out of the car. I was still in my uniform, but it was all wrinkled, and my eyes were all red. "I'm a mess."

"No. No, you're not."

I sat down next to Joey and collapsed into his arms.

Unaware

*J*une had told me that part of the reason I detached myself was that real life was too uncomfortable, and I suppose she was right. Take social situations, for instance. I couldn't stand the awkward silences or the grammatical flaws. I was aggravated by the petty discussion topics and the exaggerated dramatics of teenaged girls. I couldn't believe that I was actually one of them.

I was doing pretty well at keeping myself occupied during school. I got all my homework done during the school day and sat in the Room only when the Trinity weren't there. It was two weeks away from winter break, and MUN meetings were on a break until second semester.

I ran into Courtney in the bathroom one day. When I

walked in, I heard her voice drift over from one of the stalls. "I know!" she said, aggravated. I thought there might be another person in the stall with her, but then I realized that she was only talking on the phone. "But Marisa, I'm doing better in science this year," Courtney said.

So it was Courtney who had failed science, which meant that it was Courtney who had gotten a boob job. But more than that, it meant that Courtney, the one girl in the Trinity who had seemed most genuine about joining MUN, had really only joined because her stepmother had forced her to. I bet that Aaron didn't know about the plastic surgery. I wondered what would happen if he found out. Would it be so wrong for me to casually slip that Courtney Gross had gotten her boobs done? After all, she had been spreading rumors that I was a slut, no doubt with the help of Kim and Alissa.

Tea Party

I had to make an appearance at the mandatory Junior Class Winter Tea on Saturday afternoon. The tea was held at the sprawling Brentwood mansion of Autumn Fielding, a ballerina in my class with whom I had little contact. The invitation emphasized that there would be very little parking available, so my mom dropped me off on her way to a location shoot. Unfortunately for me, she was going to be busy for at least two hours, so I wouldn't be able to leave the tea until, at the earliest, five o'clock. I braced myself and tried to put on a happy face.

Everyone was dressed up and chitchatting over cups of tea, delicate miniature scones, and strawberries and cream. The party frocks and peacoats made me almost forget that we were, in fact, in Los Angeles. Some of Whitbread's traditions seemed to be directly lifted from East Coast prep schools. I stood by a cluster of girls to whom I rarely spoke and made small talk about winter break plans and the difficulty of last week's biology test. The truth was, the girls I didn't know well were more willing to talk to me than those I did know. The first half hour went just fine, and I almost relaxed, realizing that not everyone read Facebook or knew Aaron Winters or listened to the Trinity's gossip.

But then Alissa arrived, fashionably late as always. She teetered in the door, a stick figure in a wrap dress and heels. I smiled, trying to show that I simply wasn't afraid of her. Hating this, Alissa made a beeline across the room for me.

"Becky." She looked me up and down with a scathing eye.

Kimberly, followed by Courtney, walked by me next. Kim "accidentally" bumped into me as she passed, sending hot tea sloshing out of my cup and onto the front of my white dress. "Slut," she hissed. Courtney gave me a hard look. I squinted my eyes to meet hers.

At first, I thought that leaving the party early would be a sign of weakness. To leave early would be to show that, no, I couldn't handle the whispered gossip on the other side of the room or the fingers pointing toward me as the rumors spread. But then I realized that this wasn't a game that I could win by just sticking it out to the end. This was my life, and it was my well-being that was at stake. And even if I did make it to the end of the tea party, neither the Trinity nor anyone else would acknowledge my strength. All that would happen would be that I would just feel even more beaten up. And I certainly didn't need that.

But once I decided that I wanted to leave—really wanted to leave, in fact—then there was the issue of how the hell I was going to get out of there. After another insult was whispered in my direction by Alissa as she soared across the room, I decided to text message my dad. *SOS*, I wrote. *If you get this, please come pick me up at Autumn Fielding's house. Please.* My dad had a business cocktail party that afternoon, and I doubted that he would leave it to come pick me up. Work was far too important.

"I'm so sorry to have to cut out early, but I have an event tonight," I said to Autumn, loudly enough, I hoped, that one or all of the Trinity heard. I wanted them to know that I had better places to be than at the stupid tea party. I excused myself and walked outside. My dad hadn't messaged me back; I had nowhere to go. I began to shiver. I had a shawl over my sleeveless dress, but that really wasn't helping me retain any heat. I walked far enough down the block that anyone leaving the party wouldn't see me, and sat down on the curb. Ten minutes passed. I contemplated going back inside, but the hatred on the Trinity's faces stopped me. Closing my eyes didn't help the dejection I was feeling. But because my eyes were closed, I didn't see my dad's convertible pull up across the street.

"Come on, hop in. You must be freezing," he called

through the open window.

"You came!" I said, surprised and grateful. "I thought you had that work event."

"I did. But you sent me an SOS."

That night, Dad canceled his date with Darcy and went out to dinner with me instead. I filled him in on bits and pieces of what I had been going through—excluding, for example, being called a slut. "Sweetheart, I can't believe you've been going through all this and I had no idea," Dad said. "I want to be there for you and to support you, but I can't read your mind. I have no way of knowing what's going on with you unless you tell me."

"I know. And I'm going to try to get better at telling you things and keeping you in the loop. It's just hard because, well, when you and Mom split up, I think I sort of blamed it on you. And I know that was wrong, but I thought I had to blame someone. You guys were mad at each other, and I guess I was mad at you."

"Oh, honey. Your mom and I aren't mad at each other, and neither of us wants to make you choose sides. We're still adjusting to this new life, but we are going to get it all figured out. We are. Everything might not be perfect, but it will be okay."

Okay sounded pretty perfect to me.

Speak Up

*G*ive a speech in front of the whole school—just what I wanted to do. A month before, I might have been up for it. But now, not so much. Every year, before winter break, there's an All-School Assembly recapping the highlights and events of the first part of the year. Music and dance groups sometimes do performances, the student body president makes a speech, and a few other students are also asked to speak. This year, I was one of them. I had never been asked to give one of these speeches before. Talking to the Parents Association was one thing—giving a speech to the whole school was another. Mr. Elwright had told Ms. Morton about me winning the gavel at the MUN conference and about my project of building a school in Uganda, and she was—according to Mr. E.—so impressed that she insisted I be one of the winter assembly speakers.

But the last thing I wanted was to get up on stage and be able to see the entire junior class—as well as girls in other classes—whispering and gossiping about me while I spoke. During Advisory on Friday, one of my seventh-grade advisees had approached me and asked if I was upset that my boyfriend had dumped me for Courtney Gross. I had tried to come up with a remark that would show just how over it I was, but I didn't think I'd succeeded. What struck me most about the situation was that seventh graders knew. And if seventh graders knew, that meant that *everyone* knew.

Friday morning came. I put on a freshly ironed polo shirt and made sure that my boxer shorts didn't show below my skirt. I blow-dried my hair and even put on some makeup. I wanted to look my best. I hoped that looking good would help me to feel good. I had memorized my speech but brought a printed copy just in case I needed it.

After a performance by the modern dance troupe, it was my turn. "Hi, my name's Becky Miller," I started. And then I stopped. I thought about how crazy my life had gotten this semester. I thought about my Shit Lists and my Bright Side Lists. My prepared speech seemed so stupid, so boring, and so irrelevant. And finally, for once, I wanted to say what I meant. I wanted to speak the truth and not hold back. I looked out at five hundred waiting faces, and began again.

"I was asked to speak about my accomplishments with Model United Nations this fall and about the great first semester I've had this year. But the truth is, although my MUN experience has been great, I've had kind of a rough time recently." All of the murmurs in the hall died down. It was silent, and I had everyone's attention. "This fall, I got caught up in a silly quest for popularity. I cared too much about what other people thought about me and found myself doing the opposite of what Whitbread teaches us to do—to hold firm to our beliefs and never be afraid to state our opinions. In one particular situation, I found that I shied away from voicing my opinions because I was afraid that my opinions would affect my popularity. Instead of speaking out, I took the passive route, a decision that might have cost me a very important friendship. I want to take my time up here today to say to you that I am done with being passive. I am done with not saying what I think and with trying too hard to fit in. This past month, my boyfriend turned out to be a jerk and then posted some mean stuff about me online. The day after we broke up, a girl who I thought was one of my best friends started going out with him."

I was sure that if I looked to where the Trinity were sitting, there would be a lot of activity. I knew that I could take this opportunity to mention that his new girlfriend had failed chemistry and had a boob job, but why bother? I didn't need, or want, to sink that low.

Upon hearing about my breakup and betraying best friend, a chorus of *awww*s emerged from the audience. "No," I stopped them. I didn't want them feeling bad for me. "No. It's okay." Then I added, "*I'm* okay."

Then the applause began. It quickly gained momentum until I was receiving a standing ovation from almost the entire school. Blood rushed to my face. "The most important thing I learned this semester is this: that you should never sacrifice who you are in order to conform to other people's expectations of who you should be. Whether it's at an MUN conference, where another delegate is trying to convince you to sign onto a resolution that your country doesn't agree with, or whether it's with your friends or boyfriends." I received another round of applause as I stepped off the stage. I was grinning widely, filled with adrenaline and relief. I had no idea that speaking the truth would feel so good.

Later that day, Taylor approached me in the hall. "You were really brave to say all that stuff up there today."

"I just hope you'll forgive me for, you know, that whole Facebook situation."

"It hurt me that you didn't stand up for me, but, I mean, I guess I can understand why you didn't. You know something? I always saw you as this girl who was just brimming with self-confidence."

"Really?"

"Yeah. I guess that's why I couldn't quite understand

why you wanted to be friends with *them*."

I shrugged. It flattered me that she had thought I possessed so much self-confidence, but I was trying to stop caring so much about what other people thought of me. What mattered was what *I* thought of me. Nonetheless, I was glad that Taylor was speaking to me again. She was a genuinely sweet girl who I had hurt unfairly. "So, feel free to say no," I ventured, "but would you maybe want to go out for coffee this weekend? We could go to Peet's or something?"

Taylor paused, looked me in the eye, and said, "No, I don't think so."

"Oh." I should have been expecting that. "Yeah, I understand." Taylor nodded, silent.

"I just hope you know how sorry I am. Your friendship means a lot to me, and if I could do things over, I would. . . ."

"But you can't."

"I guess I can't." I wanted to tell her that I could try to do better in the future, that I *would* do better, but I could see that she wasn't ready to believe me. And why should she? It's not like I'd been such a great friend so far.

"I should get to class," she said.

I nodded. "See you around?"

"Yeah. See ya."

I stood there for a minute, watching Taylor walk down the hallway, away from me.

Home Sweet Home (No, Really)

*M*om had decided to sell the Doheny Park apartment—once the repairs were finished, of course—and went into escrow on a house in Hancock Park, only four blocks away from Whitbread and eight blocks from my dad's house. Mom, moving fast as always, set "Immediately" as the moving date.

So we packed up our stuff from the Four Seasons and moved to South Arden Boulevard. The house was light blue with bright white shutters and a garden in the front. It felt fresh.

Just four months before, I had carried a suitcase of

possessions from my dad's house into a foreign apartment at Beach Tower. Now I was back in Hancock Park, and I was just as popular as I had been at the beginning of the school year, which is to say, not very. Taylor still hadn't forgiven me, but I'd done my best and hoped that someday we'd be friends again. Although I wasn't necessarily happy yet, I knew that someday, I would be. And even though my life was far from perfect, I had started to believe that just maybe it was actually going to be okay.

That Saturday morning, I carted boxes of books into my new bedroom as Pam Michaels and my mother walked around the house determining what the best layout for the furniture would be. My brother played video games in his room. A little past noon, the doorbell rang. It was Joey. "Hey," he said. "How are you doing?"

"Better." I was starting to actually believe in my words. "Thanks for, you know, being there for me. It meant a lot."

Joey's cheeks flushed a little. Joey was looking into my eyes so sincerely that it made me feel light-headed. "Of course. Anytime." Then he added, "Hey, um, do you want to go get lunch on Larchmont or something?"

We started off down the block walking side by side, our steps almost in rhythm. Then, slowly and gently, Joey reached out his hand to meet mine. Our fingers interlaced, and a shiver traveled up my arm. Joey turned to look at me, and I looked right back at him. I smiled, then turned back to look at the sidewalk in front of me.

Back in Hancock Park, it was almost as if I had come full circle—except not quite. Because in the past four months, a lot had changed. I had changed, and I would continue to change. Maybe my time in high school wouldn't be the best years of my life. But maybe that wasn't such a bad thing. Because if you peak at sixteen, then really, what was there to look forward to in life?

I was ready to stop looking backward, ready to stop focusing on what could have been, and ready to start focusing on what still could be.

It was my life, and I was going to own it.